Skateboard Sibby

Skateboard
SIBBY

CLARE O'CONNOR

Second Story Press

Library and Archives Canada Cataloguing in Publication

O'Connor, Clare, 1967–, author
Skateboard Sibby / Clare O'Connor.

ISBN 978-1-77260-087-2 (softcover)

I. Title.

PS8629.C622S53 2019   jC813'.6   C2018-905147-7

Cover by Rekka Bell
Edited by Carolyn Jackson

Printed and bound in Canada

Second Story Press gratefully acknowledges the support of the Ontario Arts Council and the Canada Council for the Arts for our publishing program. We acknowledge the financial support of the Government of Canada through the Canada Book Fund.

ONTARIO ARTS COUNCIL
CONSEIL DES ARTS DE L'ONTARIO
an Ontario government agency
un organisme du gouvernement de l'Ontario

Canada Council   Conseil des Arts
for the Arts   du Canada

Funded by the Government of Canada
Financé par le gouvernement du Canada

Canadä

MIX
Paper from
responsible sources
FSC® C004071

Published by
SECOND STORY PRESS
20 Maud Street, Suite 401
Toronto, ON M5V 2M5
www.secondstorypress.ca

For Mom and Olivia,
Who beautifully bookend my life.
You are resilience and hope personified.

CHAPTER 1
Starting New

My insides are getting that gross sort of carsick feeling as I step onto the schoolyard. And it's not because of the sour milk I drank by accident—thanks to Pops forgetting that I live with him and Nan now.

Yuck.

I stop walking, and Charlie Parker Drysdale strides on ahead of me. He's still talking about how I'll love living in Halifax and going to his school.

I'm not looking at him. I'm looking at the bodies popping in and out of that skateboard park, which is why my insides feel gross.

"Seriously," I say in disgust. "A new park?" I mean I used to skateboard through this schoolyard whenever we visited Nan and Pops. The yard I'm standing in and the empty lot behind the school were the only places to skateboard when I actually *had* a board.

"Yeah," says Charlie Parker Drysdale as he turns a little to the right to walk toward the park. "*Another* reason
you're going to love it here."

Nope, I say to myself. *I will NEVER love living here.*

I'd like to say that out loud, but I don't because of
what Vera told me. She was my super best friend at my
old school. She told me to follow exactly two rules when
I got to my new school. Vera said this: "First, be chill.
Being chill is how you will make new friends." But then
I said, "What new friends? Who needs new friends? And
you know I don't like rules." And then Vera said, "See,
that. *That* is what *not* being chill sounds like."

I'm new at chill. I am not new to Charlie Parker
Drysdale.

We used to spend time together whenever I visited
Nan and Pops. Now he's my next-door neighbor and my
one and only school friend. Guess that makes him my
new best friend. Maybe. Dunno. Feels kinda soon.

The closer we get to the park, the louder the sounds
get—wheels on cement, music, and voices yelling words
like *sick*, and *whoa*, and *dope*.

"Esther!" shouts Charlie Parker Drysdale. "Esther," he
shouts again and starts waving his hand. A girl wearing
a pink helmet with big stars on it smiles and rides her
scooter toward us.

"Charlie," she yells back, which is weird to hear. I

mean, I could never call Charlie Parker Drysdale just Charlie. I've tried, but he always wears a sweater-vest, and boys who wear sweater-vests should be called by their full name if you ask me. Today's sweater-vest is bright green. I always wear hoodies. Today's hoodie matches my hair, which Nan calls "sun-kissed." I just call it "light brown."

I hear Charlie Parker Drysdale say something about Esther's scooter being new. But I'm not totally listening because I'm staring at *the* biggest *most* amazing skateboard park I've ever seen.

"So sick," I whisper as my eyes travel from one end of it to the other. I'm not even sure how long I've been staring before I notice my mouth is hanging open. I'm pretty sure Vera would say it's easier to make friends when your mouth is *not* hanging open, but she hasn't seen this park. It's super dope. It has everything any skateboarder would want—handrails, half pipe, quarter pipe, a bowl, flatbars, a pyramid, ledges, and even a five-stair hubba.

I tighten my fist. Normally, when I do that at a skateboard park, I feel the front truck of my skateboard. Now, I just feel the inside of an empty fist. And that makes the carsick feeling move up my throat to make my mouth feel all watery.

"...so I don't know what his problem is," Esther continues, "but stay away from him is all."

"Huh?" I say and I turn toward Esther. She and Charlie

Parker Drysdale are standing beside a bike rack. "From who?" I ask just as Esther clicks the lock on her scooter.

She doesn't hear me.

"That's Sibby." Charlie Parker Drysdale points at me. "Just got here last night."

"Hey," I say.

"Hey," she says and takes her helmet off. Her hair is all black, except for the bottom. The tips are blue. I open my mouth to ask who we should stay away from, but then we hear shouting coming from the park. Right away, I see a boy on a skateboard getting serious height at the top of the half pipe. Another boy is cheering him on and yelling "Duuuude" every time the boy on the skateboard rides up the ramp and into the air.

"Whoa," I say, and, instead of noticing that my mouth is open, I'm noticing that it's smiling. It didn't smile much after Mom and Dad told me we were moving. And then it totally stopped smiling after I said good-bye to my skateboard.

Looking at those boys makes me feel better because I think—maybe—I could borrow a board from one of them just to take a couple of turns. Skateboarders help each other; at least they did at my old school. If they ask where mine is, I'll say something like, "Lipslide. On a rail. Snapped the deck." And then maybe they'll be like, "Sick. But too bad about your board. Here. Borrow."

And then I'll do a 50-50 grind and they'll be like, "Wow, new girl's dope."

And then Mom and Dad will be like, "Hey, Dad got his job back. We're moving back home." And then Vera and I will go buy me a new board.

"Sibby!" I hear Charlie Parker Drysdale calling. "Sibby. Come on." I look away from the park and see that he's headed toward the school's front entrance.

"Where's Esther?" I ask as I'm running to catch up with him.

"In the line," he says, "with Hannah. They're saving us spots."

I look back at the park one last time. I don't know where the boy who was skateboarding went, but he's not in the air anymore. Just seeing those skateboarders makes me think maybe it won't be so bad living here. Maybe...

Plouph!

Since I wasn't looking in front of me, I run right into Charlie Parker Drysdale's backpack. It falls off his shoulder and lands on my left foot.

"Ouch!" I say. And when I look down, I see something awful.

"Oh, no. No. No. No," I say...like that's going to erase what's staring back at me.

I hear Charlie Parker Drysdale zip his backpack open.

"A scuff," I mutter, rubbing my left shoe. "Go away,"

I say, like I can actually make something happen just by saying so. Man, I wish I could. If I could, I'd say, "Go back…to the way it was."

"What's the big deal? Your shoes have lots of scuffs," says Charlie Parker Drysdale.

"Not like this," I snap. Seriously. This can't be happening. No board. And now my red skateboard shoes have a regular scuff like…like they're regular shoes. *As if.*

I keep trying to get the scuff out. It's not working.

"Whew, nothing broken," says Charlie Parker Drysdale and I hear him zip up his backpack.

"What's not broken?" I ask and I keep rubbing.

"Sorry, Sibby. Your foot okay?" he asks, which is weird. He says it like he didn't even hear my actual question. And that makes me stop rubbing and look up. I see him staring at the line of kids. It reminds me of Dad staring at the For Sale sign on our front yard and asking how I was feeling about moving.

"Whatever," I had said.

"Maybe later," Dad muttered, which didn't make sense. But that's what happens when you're too weirded out to hear right. I don't know why Charlie Parker Drysdale is weirded out.

"Foot's fine," I snap, but then I remind myself to chill. So, I stand back up and, in a voice that sounds as chill as I can make it, I say, "What's in your backpack? Rocks?"

"No," he says. "My homework. Remember?"

"Homework?" I shout. "Already? But it's our first day. Who has homework on the first day?"

"It's like I told you," he says. "Ms. Anderson sent an email."

"Ms. *who?*"

"Wow, Sibby, did you listen to anything I said while we were walking to school?"

"Can you just tell me again?" I ask.

And, seriously, I say inside my head, *you said a whole bunch of stuff on the way here. How am I supposed to remember it all?*

"Doesn't matter," says Charlie Parker Drysdale when we reach the end of the line. "It's easy homework. We're just supposed to talk about our summer vacations."

The sour milk feels like it's crashing around inside my stomach like ocean waves smashing against rocks in a storm. My first day is starting to feel like the worst first day of school *ever*. I mean I'd rather go to the dentist than talk about my summer. No. Worse. I'd rather go clothes shopping—for a dress—than talk about my summer.

Just lie and say, "It was good," I tell myself. *And sound chill.*

"So why'd you bring rocks?" I ask. I've never seen Charlie Parker Drysdale with rocks. He's never even talked about rocks. We've talked about skateboarding.

Correction. I've talked about skateboarding. We've eaten pepperoni pizza together and watched videos of Josephine Jackson skateboarding. She's the best Under-13 skateboarder there is and even has her own video channel. She goes by Jackson Jo. So dope.

"It's not rocks," says Charlie Parker Drysdale as he scans the line of kids in front of us. "It's…It's…"

"It's what?" I ask.

And then he says, "Uh-oh."

"Can too!" we hear Esther shout. Her voice doesn't sound very chill. There are lots and lots of kids in the line. Esther and another girl are halfway between its beginning and the very end where I'm standing with Charlie Parker Drysdale. They're talking to the two boys I saw at the skateboard park.

"Hey," I say. "Are those boys—?"

"Sibby," Charlie Parker Drysdale turns to me really fast, "I need to tell you something—"

"Hey," says one of the boys and then he gets out of line, drops his board, and starts riding toward us. The boy who was cheering him on comes too.

"Ineedtotellyou…aboutthoseboys," says Charlie Parker Drysdale very fast.

And now he totally does not sound chill either.

CHAPTER 2
Hello Trouble

A soccer ball flies through the air above the line of kids. It goes right past the sign on the front door of the school announcing—in big letters—Michael G. Murphy Elementary. A woman, who I think is a teacher, watches the ball go and calls to a girl in line to "collect it and bring it back."

Everyone watches the girl run after the ball, everyone, that is, but Charlie Parker Drysdale, Esther, and me. We are watching the two boys from the skatepark skate right for me and Charlie Parker Drysdale. When they get close, they both lean back on the tail of their boards, come to a stop in front of us, and then jump off. Then they pop the noses of their boards into their hands. Weird. It's like they're in a synchronized skateboarding video.

"Hey," says the boy who was getting serious air back at the park. But he's not saying it like, "Hi, how's it going? Welcome to our school. Wanna borrow my board?"

Nope. What I hear in his voice makes me think I'm about to break Vera's second rule, which was "Avoid trouble." But then he walks right by me like I'm invisible, so maybe keeping rule number two won't be so hard after all. Now he's nose to nose with Charlie Parker Drysdale.

Seriously? I think to myself. *Why's he getting all up in Charlie Parker Drysdale's face like that?*

I look at the other boy like I'm saying, "What the…?" He just looks back at me like he's all confused about what's about to happen.

"Not cool, Dude," says the boy in Charlie Parker Drysdale's face and he points behind him to where Esther is standing. "No line cutting."

"He didn't," says Esther who is now standing beside us. "*I* was saving spots, Freddie."

Right, I think to myself. *Esther was saving spots. So, why bug Charlie Parker Drysdale about it?*

And then the boy Esther called Freddie steps back.

Okay. Good. He's backing off.

But instead of going back to his place in line, he looks Charlie Parker Drysdale up and down.

"And that's not cool either," says this Freddie kid and he's pointing at Charlie Parker Drysdale's sweater-vest. "You look like a Muppet."

A Muppet? Charlie Parker Drysdale only ever looks like…well, Charlie Parker Drysdale.

The second boy is now looking the way I felt when Mom made me wear that stupid dress with the really tight band around the middle—super uncomfortable.

I fold my arms across my chest and make a you-don't-scare-us face. I mean how crazy is this? Who does this kid think he is?

Stay chill, I tell myself. *Charlie Parker Drysdale will say something to this total jerk-face Freddie kid. Just wait.*

Nothing.

Say something, I yell inside my head.

Still nothing.

Come on. I'm bursting.

Waiting for Charlie Parker Drysdale to tell the total jerk-face in front of him to back off is almost as hard as waiting for Dad to admit the real reason we moved. "Just tell the truth!" I wanted to shout at Dad but couldn't. It feels mean to shout at someone who walks around looking like he got the wind knocked out of him from the biggest slam of his life.

Charlie Parker Drysdale looks down at his bright green sweater-vest. He's not saying anything.

It's really hard *not* to talk when no one else is. I can't stand it. I talk to myself.

Stay chill. Avoid trouble. Stay chill. Avoid trouble. Stay chill…I say it over and over until…

"Um…I like it, Freddie," says Charlie Parker

Drysdale. "And I'm pretty sure Muppets don't even wear sweater-vests, at least not like mine anyway."

"Pretty sure I saw a movie where there was a Muppet wearing one," says Freddie.

Muppets? You're talking about Muppets? Can't you see what this jerk-face is doing?

There is only one thing that needs to be said. But Charlie Parker Drysdale just keeps looking down until Esther says, "Come on, Charlie. The line will start moving soon, and Hannah's saving our spots. Let's go." Esther starts to walk back to Hannah, and Charlie Parker Drysdale tries to follow her.

GO? What? You're just gonna let him get away with that?

"When you come to school tomorrow," says Freddie like he's some kind of king boss of everyone, "no Muppet clothing."

And then he gets in Charlie Parker Drysdale's face. Again.

My arms fall loose.

"That's it." I step between Freddie and Charlie Parker Drysdale.

"Charlie," calls Esther from the middle of the line. "You coming?"

"Um, nope. I'll catch up," he says. "I think."

I'm looking straight at Freddie, but I don't see a skateboarder. I see a bully. And a bully is the reason I'm living in this stupid town, going to this stupid school, and missing my super best friend. I can't stand bullies, and *I* won't let this one win.

"Back off," I demand.

Freddie is staring at me, and I'm staring right back. I don't know what he's seeing, but I'm seeing someone who isn't so good at being chill or avoiding trouble either.

CHAPTER 3
In or Out?

For weeks leading up to the Charlottetown Skateboard Invitational last month, I practiced all kinds of tricks: flips, grinds, and slide tricks. I even practiced grab and air tricks.

The trick I couldn't make was a backside bluntslide. It's super hard. It's also Jackson Jo's best trick. I mean she can do anything, but watching her do a backside bluntslide is like watching someone fly. She says to do it on a ledge first because you don't have to pop out. But I saw her backside bluntslide on a quarter pipe. She held the slide for four whole Mississippis.

At the Invitational, I landed a backside bluntslide on a quarter pipe, too. But I barely held the slide for half a Mississippi before I popped out and had a totally sketchy landing. It wasn't enough to beat Ian McFarlane, but I did beat Evan Rothsay. And the look on Evan's face when I beat him and came second to Ian is the same look Freddie has right now. Total shock.

"Who. Are. You?" he asks.

"Yeah," says the boy who was at the park cheering on Freddie. "Who *are* you?" He says it like he actually wants to know.

They're both still holding their skateboards by the noses.

"Sibby," I answer.

"*Sippy?*" says Freddie. He laughs and gives the other boy a high five. The other boy doesn't look so into the high five.

"That's not what I said...*Fartie*," I say.

Freddie stops laughing but the boy with him starts. But then Freddie gives his sidekick a you-better-quit-laughing-because-she's-making-fun-of-me sort of stare.

"What?" says the boy to Freddie. "It was funny."

Freddie keeps staring at him.

"Okay, okay, whatever." And the boy stops laughing.

"Never saw you before," says Freddie. "And the name's Freddie, not Fartie."

"It's my first day," I say. "And the name's Sibby, not Sippy."

"Where'd you come from?" asks the other boy.

"Charlottetown," I say. "And who are you?" I stand up as straight as I can. I heard Mom tell Dad that's how you deal with bullies. You stand up straight and show confidence. Too bad Dad didn't listen. If he had, none of this would be happening.

"Jake," says the boy. He lifts his fist into the air like he wants to connect with mine. I lift mine too.

"Dude?" says Freddie in a stop-being-so-nice sort of voice.

"What? She's new. That's it," says Jake. We bump fists.

Freddie tucks his blond curly hair behind his ears and asks me, "What's your deal?"

I fold my arms across my chest and am about to say, "What's yours?" but before I get the words out, Charlie Parker Drysdale starts blabbing.

He says, "Sibby's from PEI. Hey," he points to their boards, "she skateboards too. She was even in a competition. Now she lives with her grandparents because her dad lost his job building houses and they had to sell their—"

And then I remember why I only ever talked to Charlie Parker Drysdale about pepperoni pizza and skateboarding.

He has a *very* big mouth.

"Hey," my arms fall loose, and I sputter, "stop talking. And how do you even know all that?"

"Your nan told one of my moms," he says. "She said to be extra nice to you because—"

"Extra nice?" I shout and I put my hand straight up, palm out. "STOP!" I mean who wants to hear someone say all the things you want to forget. And *then* say that they're being extra nice to you because their mom said so.

Charlie Parker Drysdale is definitely *not* my new best friend. Just decided.

I can't wait to tell Vera how her rules *do not* work at this school.

"Why?" says Charlie Parker Drysdale. "What's so wrong with—?"

"Just zip it." I turn my stop sign hand into one with a finger pointing straight at him.

And then he gets *that* look on his face.

It's sort of like the look Dad had when he sold our tent at our third garage sale.

"Sib," Dad had said when he was gathering the tent to give to the man who bought it, "you sure you're okay with this? Lots of good memories with this tent."

"Barely," I had said.

And then he had *that* look. Like when you've been practicing a trick over and over but you just keep bailing, and you feel like you're never going to get it right. But what was I supposed to say? "No, Dad. Stop selling everything. I want to keep the tent *and* our house, but we can't. And it's your fault."

17

I don't like being mad at him, but I can't help it. It's good that he and Mom stayed in Charlottetown to get our things organized, at least what's left of our things.

"But what'd I say wrong?" says Charlie Parker Drysdale.

"Just quit..." I start to say, but then I remember what Vera said about being chill. I take a deep breath and sound as chill as I can when I say, "...talking. Just quit talking. Please."

"Weirdos," says Freddie.

"Hey," says Jake to me. "Why do you care about a stupid sweater-whatever?"

"Vest," I say. "It's a sweater-vest and why does he?" I point my nose toward Freddie.

Freddie, Jake, and Charlie Parker Drysdale are all staring at me.

I really wish I still had my skateboard. Standing on it gives me what Mom says Dad lost: confidence. My insides are feeling gross again.

"What competition were you in?" asks Freddie.

The thing about insides is that Freddie can't see them. So, I make my outsides show confidence.

"Charlottetown Invitational," I say.

"Never heard of it," Freddie smirks. And then he looks over at the skateboard park again.

Evan Rothsay had a look exactly like that when he

thought he could beat me. Boy skaters are always thinking they can beat me.

Freddie's look tells me he's thinking about daring me to skate against him, but I don't want to. I can't. I don't even have a board.

"Sibby came second," blurts Charlie Parker Drysdale.

I stare at him and just before I can give him a signal to zip it, he says, "And she won those shoes. Cool, right?"

"Second," laughs Freddie. "Big deal. Probably only her and some other loser competing anyway, which means she was *last*."

"What's going on over there?" says the woman standing at the front entrance of the school.

Everyone but me says, "Nothing." I'm too busy trying to keep my insides calm to answer. This Freddie kid is really making me mad.

When the woman looks away, he lowers his voice and says, "Let's see if you can out skate *me* with the whole school watching." He points to the skateboard park. "After school?"

I want to yell "It's on!" but I can't. I don't have a board. And it's not like I can borrow one from Charlie Parker Drysdale. And I sure can't beat Freddie with Esther's scooter.

When I don't answer Freddie says, "See. Nothing but a poser."

"Hey," I step toward Freddie. "I'm *not* a poser," I tell him.

Then we hear the woman at the front entrance of the school say, "Welcome back, everyone."

Freddie's smirking at me like he's already out skated me.

"You in or out?" he says.

"Are you ready to come inside?" shouts the woman.

The kids in line shout, "YEAH!" Some are even jumping up and down.

"Well?" says Freddie.

I don't answer.

"Didn't think so," he says and he starts to walk away. I feel like I've been bullied. And bullies have caused me enough trouble.

"IN!" I shout before Freddie gets out of earshot.

CHAPTER 4
It's Not About a Sweater-vest

Freddie and Jake go to the middle of the line and do exactly what they told me and Charlie Parker Drysdale we couldn't. They cut. And no one stands up to them. Bullies always win.

"Let me guess," I say to Charlie Parker Drysdale. "Freddie and Jake are in our class?"

"Uh-huh," he says. "Freddie MacPhee and Jake Kwan. I've been in the same class with Freddie since first grade. Jake just moved here last year. He's okay, but Esther said Freddie was acting kinda mean at the park before we got there."

"What's his deal?" I ask.

"Don't know," he answers. "Freddie's been a jerk before, but that's the worst I've ever seen him."

Charlie Parker Drysdale wipes his forehead.

"Look." He shows me his hand as the line starts to slowly move forward. "That whole thing made me sweat."

My eyes go from Charlie Parker Drysdale's sweaty hand to his shiny black hair. It's held in place with some kinda gel. I never use gel. When my bangs fall into my eyes, I just blow air at them. *Fffffffpp*.

"Sibby, I know you're a good skateboarder and everything, but so is Freddie." He takes a cloth from his backpack and wipes the sweat off his hand. "He's like, the best in our school."

"Doesn't matter," I say. "I won't be living here or going to this stupid school for long. When Dad finds a new job, we're going back home."

"That's not what your nan told my moms," says Charlie Parker Drysdale. "She said your dad might have to go away for work." He puts the sweat-stained cloth back inside his backpack and keeps talking. "She said if that happens, you and your mom will be living with your grandparents for a long time."

"Dad *will* get a new job," I snap. "Didn't like his old one anyway," I say, even though I know that's not true.

"Maybe I should just wear something that's not a sweater-vest tomorrow," he says. "Then nobody has to show up at the skateboard park and compete."

"No way," I tell him and I stop walking. "Charlie Parker Drysdale," I say quietly, "I know a few things about bullies. You can't give in and let them tell you what you can do or what you can wear. If you do, all sorts of really bad things happen. Trust me. *Really* bad."

"It's just once," he says. "And why do you care so much about my sweater-vests?"

"Ugh. It's not about a sweater-vest," I say. "It's about not getting pushed around by a stupid, idiotic, jerk-face, cheese-head bully."

"Okay, okay," he says, and the way he says it tells me I'm not being chill. "Were you bullied at your old school or something? I don't remember you being so...so... intense."

"No," I say, and we start walking up the steps of the front entrance. "*I* wasn't. But someone I know was."

"Was it your friend...um...what's her name?" he asks. "Vera? Was it her?"

I shake my head. "No," I say.

"Then who?" he asks.

"Doesn't matter," I say.

If Charlie Parker Drysdale weren't such a blabber-mouth, I'd tell him.

I'd tell him it was Dad.

I'd tell him how I overheard Dad telling Mom he felt like he was being bullied into doing things he didn't agree with in order to build houses faster. But I thought he'd just tell the bully to stop bullying. I mean why's that so hard?

Instead, he quit. He totally quit his job and we ended up selling things in yard sales. Next thing I know, a big ugly For Sale sign is sticking out of our front lawn and then Pops and I are driving over Confederation Bridge. For good. All because Dad didn't stand up to a bully.

What's even worse than that? He didn't tell me the truth. He said some made-up thing about how it was time to move on.

But we didn't move on. We just moved away.

Charlie Parker Drysdale doesn't know what happens when you let a bully push you around.

"Do you like your sweater-vests?" I ask him when we're walking inside.

"Yeah. What's not to like?" he says.

"Then keep wearing 'em," I say.

"You sure sound like you know what you're doing," he tells me.

I don't.

All I know is that *I* will never back down to a bully.

CHAPTER 5
Ghost Board

Just inside the classroom, there are lots of hooks for coats and backpacks. There's also a big yellow shelf that looks like a dresser without drawers. A few helmets, including the one Esther was wearing, are sitting on the very top. And there are exactly three skateboards on three separate shelves. Two of the skateboards have a black deck like my old one and look like the ones Freddie and Jake were holding. The third is sticking out of the shelf a little and has a wider deck with a design on it. And it has RageG3 wheels, which are really good for sliding.

Heyyy, I say inside my head. *Who owns that?*

Just thinking there is another skateboarder in the class makes me feel better. I mean maybe this one isn't a total jerk. In my old classroom, we all had our very own shelves with our names on them so we'd all know who owned what. Not here. I hang my backpack on a hook. I miss having my very own shelf.

The floor in the classroom looks shiny clean, but the smell of something stale fills my nose. It's like I'm breathing in a stack of really old library books. Even though sunshine is streaming through the big windows along the wall on the other side of the room, the lights above are super bright. The back wall of the room is filled with posters that say things like *Be a friend*, and *Listen*, and *Respect is best*. The wall opposite the windows and closest to where I'm standing has a poster that says *Every day is a good day to be kind*. I'm betting the person who wrote those posters never had someone like Freddie in their class.

Desks and chairs are all lined up one behind one another in four rows in front of me. There's a big desk at the front with a whiteboard behind it. At my old school, the desks and chairs weren't in rows. They were pulled together to make groups of six to a table. Vera was in my six. I think it's better to have groups of six. Definitely.

"Charlie, Sibby," I hear Esther's voice. She's waving at us from her desk and pointing at a couple of empty desks behind hers.

I follow Charlie Parker Drysdale but stop when the same woman from the schoolyard, the one who told Freddie, Jake, Charlie Parker Drysdale, and me to come inside, tells me her name is Ms. Anderson. She tells me she is my new teacher and asks me to follow her to the front of the class.

Charlie Parker Drysdale is now sitting behind Esther. Hannah, the girl with the big glasses who was in line with Esther is now in the seat behind Charlie Parker Drysdale. They're all smiling at me.

"Everyone, I want to introduce you to a new student. She's just moved here from…"

Ms. Anderson waves her hands as she talks. She points toward me with her left hand. I notice her pinkie finger is crooked. I've never seen such a bent pinkie before. It's so crooked it makes me look at my pinkie fingers.

Nope. Not crooked.

My eyes then look down at my red skate shoes.

There are lots of scuffs on them but the one from Charlie Parker Drysdale's backpack is the one I notice most. It makes me feel like I'm not a skateboarder anymore, just a regular kid with regular scuffs. My insides start feeling gross again.

I look at Esther's feet and then at Charlie Parker Drysdale's. They're both wearing what Charlie Parker Drysdale calls "loafers." I call them "no-laces shoes." I think shoes should have laces. I start to look around at everyone else's shoes. A mix of laces and no-laces. And only two pairs of skateboard shoes. I look at the legs and then the faces those skateboard shoes belong to: Freddie and Jake.

Who is the other skater? I wonder. *I mean who would*

leave that board there if they weren't in this class? A board without a skateboarder is spooky, it's like...a ghost board.

"...so please welcome Sybil Henry to our classroom," says Ms. Anderson as she claps.

Everyone—except Freddie—claps too. He whispers something to Jake who is sitting behind him and they both laugh.

"You may take a seat, Sybil," says Ms. Anderson. I look around. There is only one seat left. It's across from Hannah, which is okay. But it's behind Jake, which is not okay. But, at least I don't have to sit behind, across from, or in front of Freddie.

"Please stop snickering," Ms. Anderson tells Freddie and Jake. Jake stops but Freddie doesn't, which makes Ms. Anderson tell me to stop walking.

"I have an idea," she says. "Jake, please move back a seat." And then Ms. Anderson lifts her crooked pinkie hand into the air, points her index finger in the worst direction possible, and tells me to take the seat *right* behind total jerk-face Freddie's.

"Well that figures," I say without realizing that it came out louder than I meant.

"What's that, Sybil?" asks Ms. Anderson.

"Nothing," I say. "But, Ms. Anderson?"

"Yes?"

"Can you please call me Sibby? Everyone does."

"Please take your seat, Sybil," she says. Ms. Anderson is not such a good listener.

"Cool. Now you're right across from me," says a smiling Charlie Parker Drysdale.

I nod and say, "Uh-huh." And, for a second, I think maybe it won't be totally horrible.

But then, just as I am about to walk past Freddie, he sticks his foot out.

Stupid bully.

I lift my foot high enough to go over his.

"Joke's on you," I whisper as I bring my foot down.

"Ahhhh!" Freddie yells.

Everyone turns toward Freddie, including Ms. Anderson. "What's the matter, Frederick?" she asks.

There's lots of laughing and snickering. I think it's because Ms. Anderson calls Freddie *Frederick.*

"Sy...*bil* stepped on my foot," he says.

"Sorry, Ms. Anderson," I say. "Stepping on Fred... *erick's* foot was an accident."

Except it wasn't.

"Didn't hurt," says Freddie, holding his breath.

"Did too," I whisper.

"Fine then," says Ms. Anderson, and she goes back to moving papers around at the front of the room.

"Man, you're gonna lose big after school," whispers Freddie. "And *every*one will be there to watch. Everyone!"

"Do I look worried?" I whisper back. "Because I'm not."

Secretly, I am pretty worried. I mean I don't even have a board. I look behind me at the shelf with the ghost board.

Or do I?

And then I hear Vera's voice inside my head saying, *Sibby. Don't. Just. Don't.*

CHAPTER 6
My Summer? Don't Ask

The rest of the morning Freddie is on his best behavior. He says "Yes, Ms. Anderson" and "No, Ms. Anderson" a lot.

Jake barely talks, except during English. He seems to know all the answers.

Ms. Anderson asks for volunteers to tell the class what they did for summer vacation. I absolutely do *not* raise my hand, but Charlie Parker Drysdale does.

"It's important to think back on happy memories," says Ms. Anderson. She looks at Freddie when she's talking. "They'll make you feel good, like on a cold winter's day when you miss the warm sunshine. Recalling a happy memory of playing on the beach on a beautiful day helps. At least it does for me. Charles, let's start with you."

"We went to visit my uncle in Toronto," says Charlie Parker Drysdale. He doesn't talk much about Toronto or his uncle. He mostly talks about the Ontario Science Centre.

He holds his hands out in front of him and spreads his fingers apart when he talks.

Pinkies look normal.

"…and Uncle Mike even bought me this," he says and gently lifts up a weird-looking brown rock. "It was in the gift shop."

"What is it?" asks Jake. He reaches across the row and touches the rock.

"It kind of looks like," starts Freddie, "…like—"

"It's dinosaur poop," says Charlie Parker Drysdale.

"WHAT?" yells Jake and he pulls his hand back. "Serious? I just touched poop?"

Everyone bursts out laughing. Freddie laughs so hard he almost falls out of his seat.

Esther is laughing too, but then puts her hands over her mouth to try to stop when she sees that Charlie Parker Drysdale isn't laughing. He's just staring at his dinosaur poop and smiling.

"Is that what was in your backpack?" I ask.

"Yep," says Charlie Parker Drysdale. "Too bad about your foot, but I'm glad it didn't hit the ground."

"POOP!" shouts Freddie, now plugging his nose, and making everyone laugh again.

"Settle down please," says Ms. Anderson, clapping twice. "Let's let Charles finish."

"It's not *real* dinosaur poop," says Esther.

"Um, no kidding," says Hannah. "The last known dinosaur was extinct more than sixty million years ago."

"Yeah, it's a replica," adds Charlie Parker Drysdale.

"A fake, then," says Hannah.

"No," says Charlie Parker Drysdale. "Well, not exactly."

"A replica is a copy," says Esther. "Like my sister's purses. They look just like the expensive ones but they're not. They're copies that look like the real thing."

"Right," says Hannah, "I know what *replica* means. Means it's a fake." Her voice sounds funny, like mine does when I have a cold.

"It's a replica," insists Charlie Parker Drysdale.

Weird, I think to myself, *because he seems madder about Hannah calling out his replica than he did about Freddie pushing him around.*

"Doesn't matter. Jake touched *poop,*" says Freddie. He starts laughing all over again.

"That's enough," says Ms. Anderson. "Charles, it sounds like you had a nice visit. Thanks for showing us your souvenir. Let's hear from someone else."

Esther waves her hand but Ms. Anderson says, "Hannah. How was your summer?"

Hannah talks about not liking this year's "potent pollen," but then she says she went to something called Debate Camp.

"I was so excited when I got in," she says. And she looks around the room. "It fills up quick."

"Serious?" says Freddie. "Sounds boring."

"Frederick," says Ms. Anderson. "I think Debate Camp sounds very interesting. Learning how to express your ideas is very important. Good for you, Hannah. What else did you do?"

Then Hannah says she helped her older brothers build a sand castle. She says there was a competition at a place called Clam Harbour Beach.

"Did you win?" asks Freddie.

"No," she shakes her head.

"Lame," he whispers.

"What kind of castle did you make?" asks Esther.

"A clam," says Hannah, and that makes everyone but Hannah laugh.

"Too bad it wasn't a dinosaur poop castle. Jake would've helped," says Freddie. Everyone starts laughing again.

"Quiet please," says Ms. Anderson. "Thank you, Hannah. Esther, what about you?"

Esther talks mostly about spending time at her family's cottage.

"And what did you do there?" asks Ms. Anderson.

"I read a lot," says Esther. "Mostly fashion magazines. And I mixed colors for painting toenails," she says.

That sounds like *the* most terrible way to spend the summer. It even makes me think maybe mine wasn't totally awful. Then I change my mind and decide that it was. It was totally awful.

"Esther's parents leave her at the cottage during the day with her sister, but her sister spends all her time on the phone with—"

"Charlie," shouts Esther.

"What'd I do now?" he says and looks at me and then at Esther and back at me.

"Stop telling other people's stuff," I say quietly. "Come on."

"But…" he says.

"And then Mom bought me a scooter so I could spend time at the new skatepark and meet more people," says Esther.

"Scooters shouldn't be allowed at a park like that," says Freddie.

"Frederick!" says Ms. Anderson. "Please don't make me ask you again to be more respectful."

"Yeah. Can't you read the poster?" I whisper and point to the wall.

"Poser," Freddie says but he doesn't whisper. "Oops," he says when Ms. Anderson looks at him.

Her face looks mad and sad all at the same time. It's like Freddie is really bugging her, but she feels sad about it. She takes a deep breath.

Take two breaths, is what I want to tell Ms. Anderson. *One is not enough when it comes to total jerk-face cheese-head Freddie.*

"Sybil," says Ms. Anderson. "Would you like to tell us about your summer?"

I wouldn't. I really, really, *REALLY* would *not* like to talk about my summer.

Everyone is looking at me.

A whole bunch of memories flash inside my head like pictures.

They go like this:

Vera's sad face when I told her I had to move.

Watching our tent be driven away in someone else's car.

Dad's face when SOLD was put over For Sale on the sign in our yard. It was like if he stared at it long enough, he could make everything different. You can't make something be different by staring at it. I've tried.

"Sybil," says Ms. Anderson again. "We would like to hear all about your summer. Could you please share a little about what you did?"

"Um…not much," I say. "Mostly skateboarding."

"You mean bailing," whispers Freddie.

Jerk-face, I want to say back, but I can't. Ms. Anderson is looking at me. She's looking like Mom does when she asks about my day and I say, "Good." She's looking at me like she wants more.

"She came second in a competition," says Charlie Parker Drysdale, and then he puts his hands to his mouth.

"Oops," he says through his hands.

"I don't want to talk about that," I say.

Just reminds me about not having my skateboard. And that makes my insides feel gross.

"I wouldn't want to talk about losing, either," whispers Freddie.

"What about moving to a new town and a whole new province?" asks Ms. Anderson. "That's a big thing. Do you want to tell us about that?"

"Um. I went camping," I lie, but I don't want to talk about moving either. I sure wish Ms. Anderson would ask someone else. She doesn't. She's still looking at me, so I say, "How about Freddie?"

I am staring at the back of Freddie's head. It tilts forward like he's looking down at his desk.

Guess he doesn't want to talk about his summer either, I say to myself.

Ms. Anderson looks at her watch and says that we've run out of time.

"Um, no," says Hannah. "We still have a few minutes."

Ms. Anderson ignores Hannah. "Dismissed until one o'clock," she says.

Ms. Anderson has blond hair just like Freddie's, except hers is really long and a little less curly. She sees me looking at her and smiles the same way Dad smiled when the guy who sold our house came to tell him and Mom the news. Dad smiled with his mouth, but his eyes were not smiling. Ms. Anderson's eyes are not smiling.

CHAPTER 7
Lunchroom Drama

The lunchroom at my old school had windows on both sides of the room. You could eat your sandwich and look outside and see trees everywhere. Once Vera and I pretended we were in a tree house. Just like my new classroom, this lunchroom only has windows on one side; except you can't see trees when you look outside, just sky and part of the skatepark.

My old lunchroom was better.

Definitely.

I look for Charlie Parker Drysdale, Hannah, and Esther. They're at the back of the room talking to a man dressed in gray overalls.

I start walking toward them when I see Jake and the same boys who were standing around Freddie when we were in the line. They're all at a table on my right.

Jake's facing me, but doesn't see me. He's looking really focused on whatever they're talking about.

"No way," I hear one of the boys say when I get closer. "Why?"

"Dunno," says Jake. "Didn't say. I don't get it. I mean that video was sick. He didn't bail once."

"Getting reviewed by Jackson Jo?" says another boy. "Dope."

I slow down.

What? Who's getting reviewed by Jackson Jo?

I mean she doesn't review just *any*body. Before I found out we were moving, Vera and I were going to send her a video of our best tricks. Jackson Jo is so good I'd do whatever she said to get better. I want to be in the Olympics. Street competition.

I walk super slow so I can hear more.

"So send another one," says another boy. "You make videos all the time."

The boy sitting beside him hits him in the arm.

"Ouch," he says. "What the…?"

"He can't send in another one," says the boy who did the hitting. "Duh. Not without knowing why she didn't like the first one."

Jake sees me. "Um, what're you doing?" he says.

"Nothing," I say. "Well…just…okay, I heard you talking about Jackson Jo."

"What?" says the boy who just got hit in the arm.

"Heeeyyyy, you're the new girl. The one who thinks she can beat Freddie." He's laughing. "You're in for some seriously sick embarrassment."

"You can't beat him at that park," says the other boy. "Or anywhere. Not even the flat bottom behind the school."

I ignore them.

"Serious," I look at Jake. "Who's getting a Jackson Jo review?"

"No one," he says. "She rejected the video I sent of Freddie. She keeps turning me down and I don't get why. The dude's good."

I bet I know why.

"Did you send it slo-mo?" I ask.

"Yeah, he did," says the boy holding his sore arm. "Why?"

"Yeah, why?" says Jake.

I don't answer at first because I'm not sure if I should tell him. I mean Jake wasn't as much of a jerk as Freddie, but helping a jerk be a jerk still makes you a jerk. But then I remember my one and only rule: skateboarders help each other.

"Jackson Jo says not to use slo-mo on every trick," I say.

"She does?" he says. "I never saw that."

41

"I watch everything she puts on her channel," I tell him. "There's an old video of hers where she talked about getting sponsored."

"He would've seen it if it existed," says one of the boys.

"Yeah, are you messing around?" says the other. "We heard what happened before school this morning."

"It's there," I say. "If Jackson Jo posted it, I've seen it. And I never forget anything she says."

Jake's looking at me like he's not sure if he believes me.

"Whatever," I say. "Believe me or don't."

"Um. Thanks." Jake nods. And he moves his hand like he's going to ask if I want to sit down when we hear Freddie's voice from behind me.

"Can't find someone to sit with, Sippy new girl?" he says.

The boys at the table, except Jake, start to laugh.

"Sibby," calls Charlie Parker Drysdale from the back of the room.

I look over and the man with the overalls is now gone. It's just Hannah, Esther, and Charlie Parker Drysdale at the back.

Hannah is waving at me.

Stay chill. I remind myself. *Avoid Freddie. Just walk away. Stay chill. You're in the lunchroom. Don't let total jerk-face get to you in front of everyone. Stay chill. Don't call him fart-face. Or a cheese-head. Don't.*

"Yeah, that's cool," shouts Freddie. "Sit with Hannah-big-eyes-banana and the rest of the losers." He's holding a bottle of water and takes the cap off.

Stay chill. Don't call him—

And then I feel something wet splash down on my red skateboard shoes. Freddie is putting the cap back on the water bottle and laughing at me. "Oops," he says in a loud voice. He's looking behind him at a man standing near the lunchroom entrance.

"You did that on purpose!" I yell.

"Total accident," he says and then he looks back at me and whispers, "or not."

"Fart-face, freak show!" I shout. And the boys at the table start to laugh and say "Ohhhh, no way" and "Burn."

"Sippy cup, Poser," he says, which makes them laugh even louder.

The man who was standing near the entrance is walking toward us.

Everything is bouncing around in my head and getting jumbled. Not having my skateboard makes it all worse. I think of Vera, but it doesn't help. Freddie takes the cap off his water bottle again and tilts it toward my shoes. I grab for it, but he moves his arm away.

"Okay, you two," says the man. Now that he's closer I can't tell if he's a man or a teenager. He doesn't look very old.

"Oh hey, Mr. MacDonald," says Freddie. "I *accidently* dropped a splash."

"Have a seat, Freddie," says Mr. MacDonald and Freddie goes back to the table where Jake and the other boys are. Everyone but Jake is high fiving him. "Not cool," says Mr. MacDonald to Freddie and his total jerk-face crew. "And not high-five worthy. Save those for something good."

They all sit back down but I can't see them because Mr. MacDonald steps in the way and then points to my shoes. "Cool skate shoes," he says. "Billings 505?"

"Um, yeah," I say. "How do you know that? Do you skate?"

"See this," he points to a big ugly bruise on his right arm. "Missed the landing on my last ollie. And that water?" He points to my shoes. "It'll dry in no time," he says. "I have a pair. Dark blue, plus a coffee stain. Sybil, right?"

"Sibby," I say.

And I start wondering if maybe the ghost board belongs to him. Maybe he put it there after he fell and forgot. *But who could forget a board like that?* I decide to ask him.

"Do you have a board?"

"Sure do," he says. But then someone calls his name

before he can say more. "Gotta go," he says. "Enjoy your lunch."

"Bye," I say and walk to where Hannah, Charlie Parker Drysdale, and Esther are sitting.

"What's wrong with Freddie anyway?" says Hannah when I get to the table.

"Who knows," says Esther. "He sure turned into a total jerk though."

"Who was that guy?" I ask. "Freddie called him Mr. MacDonald. Have you seen him skateboard?"

"He's a new teacher," says Hannah. "My dad told me. Don't know if he skateboards."

"Is your dad a teacher?" I ask.

"The janitor," she says. "He was just here. He said he had to go back downstairs and he'd meet you another time."

Esther, Hannah, and Charlie Parker Drysdale all have nice lunch bags. Mine is not so nice.

"Um, what's with the bag?" asks Esther.

"Nan told Pops to put my lunch in a sandwich bag," I explain, "but this compost bag is all he could find. Whatever. They're not used to having a kid around." And that reminds me of the sour milk I drank this morning before I knew it was sour. Pops said everything was happening so fast he forgot to get stuff, like fresh milk. Guess he forgot sandwich bags too.

Esther takes a fork, a real fork, from her bag.

"Nan and Pops?" says Hannah. "Where are your parents, Sybil?"

I look at Charlie Parker Drysdale. He looks like he is about to answer Hannah's question until he sees me staring at him.

"They're coming. In a few days," I say. "And you can call me Sibby."

"Are you really going to skateboard against Freddie?" asks Esther. "Charlie told us what happened in line."

"You don't have to, you know," says Charlie Parker Drysdale.

I don't recognize the food in front of him. It's brown and shaped like a horseshoe.

"Yes I do," I say. "I don't back down from bullies."

I point to Charlie Parker Drysdale's lunch.

"What is that?" I ask.

"Tofurkey," he says taking a napkin out of his lunch bag. "My moms say we're vegetarians now."

"You are?" I ask.

"Uh-huh," he says. "No more meat."

"Not even pepperoni on pizza?" I ask.

"Um, nope 'cause that's meat," he says. "It's okay though. My new favorite is pizza Margherita. I had it when I visited my uncle."

"Oh my gosh," says Esther. "I'm super in love with

pizza Margherita. My sister's boyfriend delivers pizza from Pizza Palace downtown. They make *the* best pizza Margherita."

"What's pizza Margherita?" I ask.

"Code for plain," says Hannah. "Just mozzarella, tomato, and basil. The ingredients are the colors of the flag of Italy."

"How do you know everything?" asks Esther. But she doesn't wait for Hannah to answer. Instead, she says, "Hey, do you guys want to come over tonight? We could totally order pizza Margherita."

"Can't," says Charlie Parker Drysdale. "Sibby's Nan invited me over after school, maybe we could order pizza there?"

I don't want plain pizza tonight, even if it looks like a flag. I've had enough newy-newness for one day and it's only lunchtime.

"Can I come too?" asks Esther.

"Ummm," I say because I don't know how to answer. I was planning to go home and call Vera and tell her how much my new school totally sucks.

Esther's smiling and looking at me like she really wants to come over.

"Okay," I say because I think saying no would crush her. "Guess Nan won't mind. Don't know about pizza though."

"Hannah?" asks Esther, which is weird, right? I mean why is Esther inviting Hannah to *my* grandparents' house?

"Can't come till later," says Hannah. "After the competition between you and Freddie, I'm going to debate team practice."

And now I'm thinking about skateboarding against Freddie again. If he's good enough to get a review by Jackson Jo, it means he's pretty good, and not just on half pipe. I don't want the whole school to see me lose. I stare at Charlie Parker Drysdale's food, but not because I'm thinking about what he's eating. I'm thinking about how weird it is that I'm thinking about losing. I never think about losing.

"Want some?" says Charlie Parker Drysdale.

"What?" I say.

"DO YOU WANT SOME?" he says louder. "Saw you staring," he passes me a piece.

"Never heard of tofurkey, either?" asks Esther. But she says it like it's a sentence and not a question. I don't know why but it makes me feel funny about admitting I haven't.

I take a piece. Chew. Open lunch/compost bag. Spit. Close lunch/compost bag.

I liked the sour milk better.

"Sorry," I say. "Needs ketchup or maybe…real turkey."

Charlie Parker Drysdale shrugs.

"I'll take a piece," says Esther. And then she points to the container of food she's eating.

"Do you want some of mine?" she asks me.

I'm totally done with new things so I point at my sandwich, "Nope. Thanks. Ham and cheese."

Then I look at Hannah's lunch. It's a pile of tangled looking yellow noodles that remind me of Freddie's hair, except the noodles have green specks. I decide *not* to ask what she's eating.

Lunches at my last school weren't this weird. I always had ham and cheese and Vera always had bacon, lettuce, and tomato. Simple.

"Are there other skateboarders in our class?" I ask.

"Just Freddie and Jake," says Hannah.

"And now you," says Charlie Parker Drysdale.

Then who owns that board? It must have been left behind.

Esther is holding a forkful of food near her mouth. "By the way, Freddie doesn't fall, so you need to be good to beat him." There's a white band in Esther's hair and it's keeping the hair off her face. My bangs are in my eyes. Long bangs are better than a haircut.

Fffffffpp. I blow air at them.

"Sibby's good," says Charlie Parker Drysdale. "I've seen her skateboard. Hey, remember last Easter? You were practicing that one trick over and over."

49

I nod. It was when I tried to learn an invert on the wooden box in the back lot behind the school.

Hey, behind the school! If that skateboard was just left behind, maybe I could use it out back. Just once.

Charlie Parker Drysdale swallows the last of his food and looks up at the ceiling like he's remembering something. "Wait a minute, so I guess I have seen you fall. A lot." He looks at me and he's smiling. "Remember that?"

"An invert is hard," I tell him. "You're basically doing a handstand and your skateboard is in the air above your head."

"Yeah, that's the one," he says and he's smiling, which makes me mad.

I mean why remind me that you saw me fall and then smile about it? I want to ask Charlie Parker Drysdale what the heck he's smiling about, but I don't feel like talking about skateboarding or Freddie anymore.

I look at the wall clock. We're not even halfway through lunch. All of this talk is making me not hungry anymore. I miss my old school. If I were there right now, Vera would be eating her usual. And she'd be wearing shoes that are actually shoes, not loafers. And she sure wouldn't be smiling about me falling.

I don't like this school…*or* the people…*or* this lunch-room…*or* fake turkey.

"I mean I just couldn't believe that you kept going

50

down over and over," continues Charlie Parker Drysdale.

"Yeah, I know but that was a long time ago," I snap. I'm getting mad because here I am talking about me falling, which is exactly what I don't want to talk about.

"I thought you'd have bruises everywhere," he says.

"Skaters fall," I say. "Even Jackson Jo says so."

"Who?" ask Esther and Hannah at the same time.

I sigh.

"She's a famous skateboarder. Wins all kinds of competitions. She can do street, tranny, and freestyle. And you should see her do a backside bluntslide. It's…"

Esther, Hannah, and Charlie Parker Drysdale are staring at me the way Vera would if I passed her a piece of tofurkey.

We need to talk about something else. Anything. Esther is chewing with her mouth open. And now I understand why Dad says never to do that.

"Hey, how come just part of your hair is blue?" I ask.

"Cause I only wanted blue tips." She's looking at me like I just asked a dumb question.

"She did it with Kool-Aid," says Charlie Parker Drysdale.

"Hair dye isn't good for you," says Hannah and she starts sniffing like she's going to sneeze.

"My sister told me how," says Esther. "She was going to help but she's in high school and she's really popular and busy…like my parents." Esther smiles, but it's the same kind of smile Ms. Anderson had earlier. The kind of smile you give when your insides and outsides don't match.

"*Achooo!*" goes Hannah. Wow. She sure is a loud sneezer.

"Sorry," she says. "Allergies. New pollen must be out."

And then she sneezes again. I'm waiting for the third one. Everyone sneezes in threes.

"Heyyy, Sibby," says Charlie Parker Drysdale as Hannah sniffs. "You could tell Ms. Anderson you've got really bad allergies and need to go home. That way you don't have to meet Freddie after school."

Hannah opens her mouth.

Ugh. Again with Freddie.

"Hey," says Esther. "That might actually work."

Why doesn't *anyone* want to stand up to a bully?

"*Achooo!*" goes Hannah for the third time. This one is even louder than the last. It's so loud that the whole lunchroom gets quiet just as I shout, "I'M NOT AFRAID OF FREDDIE!"

Lots of faces are looking at me.

"Crap," I whisper because I didn't mean for everyone to hear me.

Freddie stands up at the table where he was eating his lunch.

"Come see the new girl and me hit the park after school," he says in a loud voice. He's pointing at me. "She's the one sitting over there at the table with blue hair, big glasses, and Muppet-vest."

Mr. MacDonald starts walking toward him, which makes Freddie stop.

"Sure hope you can beat him, Sibby," says Esther to me. "I mean what if he gets worse?"

"Yeah," says Charlie Parker Drysdale, "sixth grade only just started."

I reach for my lunch/compost bag and toss my half-eaten sandwich inside.

Can't wait to tell Vera that the best part of my day was drinking sour milk.

I look over at Freddie. He and his friends are leaving the lunchroom, but just as they are about to go out the door Freddie looks at me, points to the window, and yells, "Skatepark!"

And that reminds me: Ghost board.

When we leave the lunchroom, Hannah says she's not going outside because she needs to practice debating. Charlie Parker Drysdale and Esther head toward the front door.

"You coming?" Charlie Parker Drysdale asks me.

"Nope," I say.

And then inside my head I say, *I need to practice too.*

CHAPTER 8
Snake Sense

The thing about having your super, super best friend's voice ringing in your head is that it can only help so much. I mean Vera's not here, so I can't say, "Yeah, okay, I'll stay chill *unless* I meet a total jerk-face bully," or "Yeah, I'll avoid trouble, *unless* I need to, you know, take a skateboard that isn't mine."

If Vera was here and I said that last part, I'm pretty sure she'd say, "Imma stop you right there."

And then I'd say, "It's a ghost board. Ghost boards don't have owners. Pretty sure. And, besides, I'll put it back when I'm done."

And then I can't hear her voice. I can only see her shaking her head. But then I picture her nodding her head, because, the thing is, Vera's not actually here.

I tighten my fist and it feels so good to feel the front truck of a skateboard instead of just air. I bet this ghost board misses skating as much as I do.

"You're just a loan," I tell the ghost board in a super quiet voice and then I peek out the front door. Everyone is scattered all over the schoolyard. I look toward the skatepark and I see Freddie, so that means Jake's probably there, too. And then I see a bright green sweater-vest and a girl wearing a pink helmet with stars on it standing on a scooter.

I walk calmly down the stairs and then duck around to the back really fast.

I can't believe this is actually working. I'm actually about to skateboard. Feels like years since I was on my board. Years.

I think about Vera again.

Borrowing a board isn't trouble. And I'm about to become very chill because that's what happens when a skater skates.

I decide that Vera worries too much.

Even the sound of the skateboard landing on the pavement makes me feel like, just for right now, things are normal. This skateboard is super dope. The deck is even wider than I thought when I saw it on the shelf. And it has a dope design. It's black with small white stars all over it. There are tiny flecks in the stars and they sparkle when the sun hits them at the right angle.

I skate across the empty lot and watch the sparkles.

"Sick," I say. "You have to be a board without an

owner. I mean, who would leave a board like you just lying around? Has to be someone who doesn't skate or who maybe moved away and left you behind in the classroom all summer. Whoever it was won't care that you and I are skateboarding right now. Right? Cool."

This big empty lot is perfect. The school is on one side and on the other side are houses with their backyards stretching to the lot. There are trees bunched in clumps behind me and scattered between the lot and those houses. There's way more weeds coming up through the pavement than I remember.

"Perfect," I say as I start to weave in and around those weeds like they're pylons. I'm leaning forward and backward on the board as I go. The *whrrrring* sound coming from the wheels on the pavement is like music as I head to the other side. The faster I go the more I feel the wind moving my bangs around my forehead.

There's a line of weeds straight ahead. Instead of weaving around them, I head right for them. I like being in the air, so I decide to ollie.

I snap the tail of the board just before the first weed and slide my front foot forward. I'm in the air over the tallest one. And then I'm on my way back down. The skateboard is right underneath my feet. It's super dope the way you can feel something underneath you, supporting you, even though you're not touching it.

BAM! I land.

That sound makes me smile a total smile. Mouth *and* eyes.

Repeat.

Mom and Dad would be so mad if they saw me skating without a helmet or pads.

"Promise us," said Dad when he bought my first board. "Never without a helmet."

"Sure," I had said. "Promise."

Being mad at Dad helps me feel a little less bad about breaking my promise.

I get ready for my next trick.

Kickflip.

I bend my front knee and lift the front of the board up. I slide my front foot up and flip. I catch it with my back foot. But just before I drop, I hear a noise. It's a rustling sound like someone is moving in the trees and it's coming from behind me. It makes me look up while I'm still in the air.

Instead of a BAM, I hear a clunk and a scrape. I land on my feet instead of the board and the board lands on its side.

I look behind me. Trees are moving in the wind and then I look around the empty lot. Nothing but a hopping crow.

I pick up the board.

"No scuffs," I say, as I look it over. If the ghost board does turn out to have an owner, it's not cool that I borrowed it and left scuff marks. "Nope. None."

I put the board down and decide to do a kickflip again, but then I hear the same noise. I turn really fast.

"This is getting creepy," I whisper, but again, I don't see anything.

Thing is, I feel something, just like I felt that snake last summer. Not a slithery snake, a skatepark snake. I was standing at the top of the skatepark in Charlottetown just about to drop in, but I felt like I was about to be snaked. I popped the tail of my board, grabbed the nose and turned really fast. There was Evan Rothsay's little brother Ewan, just about to drop in right in front of me like he didn't even care that it was my turn.

"Hey, no snaking," I had said. "We coulda banged right into each other. And it was *my* turn."

"Um. Sorry," he said.

"You see everyone up here?" I made my index finger go around in a circle to show that I was talking about everyone around the bowl. "They're all waiting their turn. No one likes a snake."

Some snakes, like Ewan, snake by accident. I'm feeling like I'm about to be snaked, and that it's not by accident.

"Georgie," I hear a voice from one of the houses call. "Georgie come!" And then I look through the trees and see a little black dog run toward a woman standing on her back deck.

"A dog?" I say and I'm relieved but disappointed, because it means my snake radar must be broken. Moving to Halifax really has changed *everything*.

I wish I had a watch. I don't want to go back inside, but there can't be much time left until lunch is over. I look at the big wooden box next to the stairwell leading in and out of a basement door.

It's the box I had used to practice doing an invert when Charlie Parker Drysdale said he saw me fall over and over.

I stare at it and picture myself using it to do a trick.

"No helmet. No way," I say.

But then I start thinking about Freddie. If I want to beat him, I have to do more than ollie and kickflip.

Sure would be nice to do a trick that would show everyone I'm every bit as good as Freddie. A backside bluntslide would probably shut him up once and for all.

I skate toward the wooden box and run my hand along its side.

"Wish I had wax," I say to the ghost board. Sliding along a dry ledge will make lots of noise. I doubt Freddie would hear from the other side of the school, but I can't take that chance.

Then I look down the stairwell leading to the basement

door. It's all brick and cement and the rail between the stairs is iron. One wrong twist and I could end up down there. There's a pile of dirt in the corner but it's not big enough or soft enough to break my fall.

"Sibby, no way," I hear Vera's voice inside my head.

"I could just land and pop out. No sliding," I argue like Vera's here.

"But—" I hear her start to argue.

"But you're not here," I say, and then I skateboard back far enough to give myself lots of room to get up speed. I lift my foot in the air and push off.

I'm skating toward the box and staring at the ledge.

I get closer.

"Freddie sure is good," I hear Esther saying in my head, and that makes me kinda mad. I don't like thinking about Freddie, especially when I'm about to do a trick. I shake my head to make her voice go away.

Closer.

"The dude is good." I hear Jake's voice.

"Shut up," I tell the inside of my head.

Closer.

"Poser," I hear Freddie say.

"Ugh," I say. "Go away. All of you."

I lean my body slightly forward.

"I saw you fall. A lot." Now it's Charlie Parker Drysdale's voice I hear.

"Quit it," I say as I'm in the air. As soon as my back truck hits the ledge, my back foot starts to slide right off the tail. I know I'm done so I decide to bail. Jackson Jo says learning how to bail is as important as learning almost any trick. First thing is never to try to land back on your board. If you decide to bail, commit to the bail and kick the board behind you. And when you land, let yourself roll.

I kick my board behind me. I hear it making a ton of banging sounds, so I know it's flying down the stairs.

I land on the pavement on my backside. But I can't roll. Not yet. I can barely move.

Total.

Slam.

I try to say ouch, but I can't get a single word to come out.

Wind.

Totally.

Knocked.

Out.

Of me.

Can't breathe.

I should be thinking about getting my air back, but all that goes through my head is, *What happened? I have to do it again. I can't compete against Freddie after THAT. Breathe, okay? Please breathe.*

GASP.

Wind is back. I'm so happy to be able to breathe again that I start breathing in and out really fast just because I can. I roll forward and then backward and then I get up and run down the stairs toward the ghost board. "No, no, no. Please don't be broken. Or scuffed," I mutter as I go.

It's lying deck down in the pile of dirt. I grab it and look it over. Still in one piece. No cracks or dents. But there's lots of dirt on the grip tape and some scuffs.

"This is not cool," I say. "I need to make this right."

I don't even think about it. I just push the basement door and it opens right into—darkness.

At first, I can't see a thing. I blink a few times and then I see a big open gymnasium in front of me. On the other side of it are stairs leading up to the main floor where my classroom is.

"Yesss," I say, but then I look to my right. There is an open door leading to what looks like a janitor's room.

Standing in front of that open door is Hannah.

"Uh-oh," I whisper.

"Sibby?" she says. "What are you doing here? Did you make that crashing sound? It was like someone threw a..." she looks at the skateboard I'm holding, "...a skateboard against the door."

"Um, yeah, dropped this." I hold up the board.

"Why did you come in through that door?" she asks.

"Oh, um…. New girl, you know," I lie.

"Hold on," she says. And then she asks, "I have a really good memory. I didn't see you with a skateboard before. Is that yours?"

"I…um…okay," I say because I know I'm busted. I walk closer to her. "I need you to keep a secret. For real," I tell her.

"Yeah," she says. "Okay. I think so."

"For real," I say again.

"Did you commit a crime?" she says.

"No," says my outside voice. *I don't think so…not exactly,* says my inside voice.

"Then okay," she says. "For real."

"I borrowed it," I tell her. And then I tell her the rest. All of it. Okay most of it. I leave out the part about not being sure I didn't commit a crime, since I took the board without asking.

"It's a ghost board," I insist. "Anyone can borrow a board without an owner, right?"

"Wow," she says. "That right there is a good question for a debate. But a board without an owner?" she says. "No way." And she's shaking her head back and forth. "I mean there's an explanation for everything. Someone has to own it."

"Are you going to tell?" I ask. "If not, I have to get it

back before anyone sees it's missing. But first I need to get the dirt and scuff marks off."

Hannah takes a deep breath. "You really don't know who owns it?"

"I swear," I answer. "I just wanted to practice. I have to beat Freddie at the skatepark. I *have* to win."

Hannah's eyes flicker. It's like something inside her actually caught the words that just flew out of my mouth.

"What do you need?" she asks.

My mind is racing. I don't clean my board as often as Vera does, but when I do, I use whatever she's using. Then I remember watching Jackson Jo use a…

"…a belt-sander cleaner," I say. "Hey, where are you going?"

Hannah runs through the open door beside the gymnasium, disappears, and then reappears with something that looks exactly like what I saw Jackson Jo use.

"Thanks." I start rubbing.

"My dad has everything down here," she says.

It's working. The board is already starting to look like it did when I took it off the shelf. "Hey, did you finish practicing?" I ask. "You said something about the debate team."

Just a couple more scuffs left to get rid of.

"Debating provincials are in November," she says. "But, like you, I have to win. I totally get that feeling."

"I have to beat a bully. Why do you *have* to win?"

"The prize money," she says. "It goes to a university fund. And I *have* to go to university."

"But we're only eleven," I remind her.

"My family doesn't have much money," she says. "If I don't start saving, I might not be able to go." I stop rubbing and look at Hannah's face. It looks worried.

And then I don't know why but I whisper, "I broke my skateboard. No way we can afford a new one."

"You don't have a skateboard?" she says. "Sibby. That's like…me not having books."

And then we hear voices and lots of footsteps.

"They're coming back inside," says Hannah. "Sibby, just take the board and run. Go."

"But not all the scuffs—"

"Close enough. We'll get the rest out later," says Hannah, like she can read my mind.

I run and get to the top of the stairs just in time to see kids coming through the door. I dart into the classroom. Ms. Anderson is facing the whiteboard. She doesn't hear me as I'm putting the board on the shelf. I turn it so the side with the scuffs isn't showing.

"Welcome back," I hear Ms. Anderson say.

"Uh-oh," I whisper, but then I see that she's not talking to me. She's not even looking at me. She's talking to Hannah who must've come in right behind me. I back away from the shelf and move to the side as a line of kids comes into the class. Jake's the first one.

My heart is beating really fast.

"Thank you," I whisper to Hannah as I sit down.

No one saw a thing, is what my head tells me.

But when I look out the window, my heart tells me, *Don't be so sure.*

CHAPTER 9
High Stakes

After school, Esther and Charlie Parker Drysdale walk to the skateboard park with me. At first, I thought it was nice not to have to walk there alone, but by the time we are halfway there, I am totally wishing I was alone.

They keep reminding me how good Freddie is.

"...even saw him do some kind of flip off the school stairs once," says Esther.

I've had it.

I stop walking and look at both of them. "Quit it," I say. "Quit talking about how good Freddie is."

"But he *is* good," Charlie Parker Drysdale says. "Really good."

"Um, Sibby," says Esther. She's looking over my shoulder.

I ignore her. "You think Freddie is the best skate-boarder at this school," I say. "Maybe so, but I bet Jake isn't over there telling him how good I am. Doesn't help."

"But Jake's never seen you skateboard," says Charlie Parker Drysdale. "He can't know how good you are."

"ARGH," I say. "Not the point."

"Sibby," says Esther loudly.

"What?" I say.

"Freddie is holding his skateboard," she says.

"So?"

"So," she says, "it reminds me—shouldn't *you* have a skateboard? I haven't seen you with one all day."

I take a deep breath.

"Oh, yeah," says Charlie Parker Drysdale. "Where's yours?" And then he points over toward the park. "And your helmet, knee pads, and elbow pads? The skateboard park rules say you can't skate without proper equipment."

"The skateboard park has a rules sign?" I say. "Didn't see it before." Skateparks should not have rules.

"Of course it does," says Charlie Parker Drysdale, like he'd know about skateparks. "So? Where's your board?"

I open my mouth, but nothing comes out. I try again. Nothing.

It wasn't this hard to tell Hannah what happened to my skateboard. Why is it so hard to tell Charlie Parker Drysdale and Esther?

"Sibby?" says Charlie Parker Drysdale. "Where is it? Where's your board?"

I look over at Freddie. He's waiting for me, expecting me to have my own board. There's no way out of this.

"Guess you're about to find out anyway," I say.

"Well that doesn't sound good," says Esther.

"I don't have one," I toss my hands into the air. "Anymore. I don't have a board anymore."

"Sure you do," says Charlie Parker Drysdale. "I've seen it."

"I don't," I say. "It broke." And then my insides feel like they're on their way up to my throat again. Saying that at a skatepark, where you are about to go one-on-one with a total jerk, sure feels harder than saying it in an empty gymnasium with someone like Hannah. She gets what it's like to not be able to buy stuff.

"Whoa," says Charlie Parker Drysdale, and he just stares at me. "Why didn't you tell me that before? I mean you always had a board. You love skateboarding. And what about being in the Olympics?"

I look over at Freddie. He's standing there with an I'm-a-better-skateboarder-than-you look on his face. Jake is with him and there are lots of kids from our class there too.

"Dunno," I shrug. "Whatever."

I sure don't feel like competing against Freddie, or anyone.

"Um, no board is a big problem," says Esther, and she says it in a way I don't like. She sounds the way Pops told me I sounded last night when Nan asked if I was nervous about starting school. Pops said I "had a bad tone" when I said "Don't really care."

"You didn't get another one?" asks Esther. And then she answers her own question. "Oh yeah. Forgot that your dad doesn't have a job."

I look at Charlie Parker Drysdale. "That," I point toward Esther, "*that* is why I don't tell you stuff. You blab. Not cool."

"Why?" he says. "She asked. What was I supposed to say?"

"Say, 'I don't know,'" I tell him. "Or don't say anything. Try that some time."

I'm the only one who's allowed to say my dad doesn't have a job and that we had to move because of it.

"What about your mom?" says Esther. "Doesn't she have a job?"

"No," I say, and I'm starting to feel kind of hot.

"Oh," says Esther. "So that's why you moved in with your grandparents."

And she says it like she gets it. Like she gets what happens when you have to sell your house and leave your super, super best friend and move away. Like she gets what it means to break your skateboard and know you can't ever get another one. There's no way that she, Ms. My-parents-have-jobs-a-house-and-a-cottage understands how *any* of that feels. *No way.*

"It's like I said," says Charlie Parker Drysdale, "I can cool it with the sweater-vests. Then no one has to do anything."

Things are getting jumbled in my head again.

"Hurry up!" yells Freddie.

Freddie acting like a bully makes me forget I don't have a board. I slow down and yell, "I'll get there when I do!"

That makes someone in the crowd behind Freddie gasp. I think about Dad and wonder if he was afraid of the bully at work and that's what made him quit his job.

"Look," Freddie yells again. "New girl brought her friends, Sweater-vest Charlie and Blue-hair Esther. And, hey, here comes Big-eyes Hannah."

Hannah is running toward us.

Freddie checks me all over like he's actually looking for something. He says, "Um, you forget something?"

I look over his shoulder and down into the skatepark. Then I peek through the crowd of people and I see the Skatepark Rules sign Charlie Parker Drysdale was talking about.

"I'm waiting," says Freddie.

"For what?" I hear Esther say.

"For new girl to tell me where her *skateboard* is!" he yells. "Duh."

Freddie turns to Jake and the kids around him and says loudly, "Told you. A poser."

Jake doesn't laugh but the other kids do.

"I'm no poser!" I shout.

"Then where is it?" says Freddie. "Where's your board?"

My mind is racing. *What am I going to do?*

"Hah," shouts Freddie. "I knew it."

I stand up straight like Mom said to, but it doesn't help this time. Then I remember what Charlie Parker Drysdale said was one of the park rules. I look past Freddie and start reading the sign.

The first rule is that no one under the age of eight is allowed to skate unsupervised.

Blah, blah, blah.

Then I see it. It's the third rule down. And I know exactly what to do.

"Doesn't matter," I say. I point to the rules sign. "Rule three. Says I can't skate without a helmet, knee and elbow pads."

"What?" says Freddie.

"Yeah," says Hannah. "Sibby's right. Too bad. Skate another time. Let's go. Can't break park rules."

"Yeah," adds Charlie Parker Drysdale. "Too bad she

left everything at home…in a box…with lots of tape over it and…"

I stare at him and mouth, "Zip it."

He gives me a thumbs up.

"Then how did you think you were gonna skate?" Freddie starts. "Is this a joke? Were you faking it this whole time? Knew you were just a poser."

I can't let total jerk-face get away with being a bully and telling everyone I'm a poser.

"I'll use yours," I blurt and I point to the one in his hand.

"No way," says Freddie.

"You afraid I'll beat you with your own equipment?" I ask.

Voices from behind Freddie say, "Whoa" and "Oh, snap" and "Burn."

"Now who's sounding like a poser?" I say, but I wish I hadn't. I mean, I totally bailed behind the school and I don't get why. I'm really not sure I can beat him.

"Dude," says Jake. "Let her use it."

"Fine," says Freddie. "Use it then." He's smirking again. "But the bet just changed."

"To what?" I ask.

"When I win, I get your crap shoes."

"What?" I say.

I can't bet my shoes.

73

"What're you going to do with Sibby's shoes?" asks Hannah. "You already have a nice pair."

She's right. Freddie's skate shoes are like new. They're black with cool bright green laces.

"She thinks she's so good because she won some competition in some small place. When I beat Sibby, that means I'm better than her *and* everyone in Charlottetown. So, when I win, those shoes are mine. Is it a bet?"

"Hold on," says Hannah. "What does Sibby get when *she* wins?"

"What do you want?" asks Freddie. "Not that it's going to matter."

"Your skateboard," says Charlie Parker Drysdale and he smiles at me.

Everything is happening so fast. I'm still thinking about my shoes.

"No chance," says Freddie.

"Scared you'll lose?" Esther asks.

Freddie looks at me like he's not sure he can win, but then his face changes.

"Okay," he says. "My board for your shoes. Let's do it. Bet?"

Everyone is waiting for me to answer. I can't let a bully take one more thing from me, but I can't back down. My mother says I never do, even when I should.

"Bet," I say, but I sure don't like these stakes. They're pretty high.

CHAPTER 10
It's On. No, It's Off

There are so many kids around the skatepark. I have to zone them out. I mean they're probably all here to cheer on jerk-face, except Hannah, Charlie Parker Drysdale, and Esther.

"Drop in, ollie on the flat, kickflip, rock to fakie. Simple," says Freddie. Everyone looks confused.

"Easy," I say, and it actually is. I've done all those tricks before. But I keep thinking about how I bailed behind the school. I mean what if I do it again on an easy trick? That's worse than bailing on a hard one.

And then Freddie says, "Whoever bails loses. If it's a tie—and it won't be—we do a…"

Just don't say backside bluntslide. Don't say backside bluntslide. Don't say backside bluntslide.

Freddie is staring at me and it's like he's inside my head when he says, "…backside bluntslide. And *if* you," he points his finger at me, "don't bail and actually land the trick, it'll come down to whoever slides longest."

He's smirking again. I'd like to land a half cab on that smirky-jerky face.

But why did he pick that trick? I mean, I didn't tell anyone here that I've only landed that trick once. And, even then, I barely held the slide for half a Mississippi.

And then I remember that there is someone I told.

"Hey, not that one," says Charlie Parker Drysdale. "I told you, she...uh-oh."

"Charlie," says Esther with a groan. "Seriously."

And then I look at Charlie Parker Drysdale. He turns his hands palms up and lifts them both in the air. "Slipped out."

Esther is shaking her head.

"Okay with you?" says Freddie, not really asking.

I don't answer. I just put out my hand.

Rock, paper, scissors.

"One, two, three," says Freddie.

We both do paper.

Again.

"One, two, three," I say.

Scissors for me, Freddie does rock. He wins.

Third time.

"One, two, three," we both count.

In my head, I'm thinking rock, but my hand makes paper.

Freddie does scissors.

He wins.

Shoulda gone with rock. What is wrong with me?

"Hah," says Freddie. "I'll go first. Show you how it's done."

"Just go already," I say.

Freddie gets on his board and does a drop in.

He's goofy-footed. I skate regular.

Freddie is on the flat and getting ready to ollie.

"Go, dude!" yells one of the boys who was with him at lunch. Another one holds out a smart phone connected to a small round speaker. Music starts playing and he turns the volume up.

Jake is holding up his phone taking a video as Freddie is getting ready to ollie.

He's in the air.

Wow, he's got serious height.

BAM.

Freddie lands the ollie.

"Nice," I say. I mean I'm hoping he bails, but skaters cheer for each another. That is the only rule that should be on the Skatepark Rules sign. That and No Bullies Allowed.

Esther and Hannah are staring at Freddie. Esther's head is bouncing up and down to the music. Charlie Parker Drysdale is pacing back and forth.

Freddie ollies again and this time he flips his board and stays over it like it's nothing.

BAM.

He lands the kickflip.

"What's next?" says Charlie Parker Drysdale. "I can't look."

"Rock to fakie," I tell him.

"Almost there," yells Freddie. Somehow his annoying voice travels over the music and cheering and comes right up into my eardrums.

He heads for the quarter pipe.

"What's a rock to fakie?" asks Charlie Parker Drysdale. He's facing the sign instead of the park where Freddie is skateboarding.

"You have to look for me to tell you," I say.

He turns and looks at Freddie who is on his way up the ramp.

"He needs to get the front of his board over the coping," I tell Charlie Parker Drysdale.

"Coping," he says. "Barely."

"No, no," I say. "*The* coping. It's that round metal at the top of the ramp."

Freddie pops the nose of his board up and over the coping.

Bail. Bail. Bail, I am saying inside my head.

But then he brings the nose of his board back up and rides back down the ramp fakie.

"Niiiiceeeee," shouts Jake.

"What happened?" asks Charlie Parker Drysdale.

"He did it," I say. "And that means it's my turn."

And, for some reason, I already feel like I've lost.

I wait for Freddie to come back so I can put his equipment on, but he doesn't. He stays on his board, lifts the nose into the air, and turns really slow to face the opposite side of the park. At first, I don't know why he's doing that, but then I see a wooden ledge. I know exactly what he's about to do and I don't like it. Not one bit.

"Ohhhh," I hear. "SICK," shouts someone from behind Jake.

"What's going on?" asks Esther.

"Hey, new girl!" shouts Freddie. His board is facing the ledge, but his head is turned to face me. "You think you can beat me? Think again."

He points at the ledge in front of him.

"WHOA," shouts Jake. "Is he gonna do a...he is... no way."

The guys behind Jake are jumping up and down.

"*What?*" I hear Esther and Charlie Parker Drysdale say at the same time.

"What's going on?" asks Hannah.

"He's not waiting for a tie," I say. "He's gonna do a backside bluntslide. And that means I have to do it too."

Freddie skates toward the ledge. He's up. He lands his back truck on the ledge.

He's sliding. Still. Sliding. He lands.

BAM.

Freddie's friends are jumping up and down.

He did it. And he slid half the ledge. I don't know how many Mississippis that is, but I'm pretty sure it's more than I can do.

And now he's running toward me and pointing.

"Beat that," he says. Freddie's eyes are big and excited. He's jumping up and down in front of me.

"Here," he holds out his skateboard and then stands still long enough to remove his helmet, elbow and knee pads.

"Take them, new girl," he says and passes me his equipment.

I can do this. I can do this. I tell myself. But, saying it over and over doesn't make it stick. My insides feel funny. And it's not because of sour milk this time. It's not even so much about a feeling I *have* as it is about one I don't have. It feels like that slam in the back lot knocked way more than air out of me. And whatever went away hasn't come back.

I.

Feel.

Like.

A.

Loser.

Hannah, Esther, and Charlie Parker Drysdale are chanting, "SIBBY. SIBBY. SIBBY." But then Freddie starts chanting even louder, "SIPPY, SIPPY, SIPPY."

I drop in. I skate along the flat and stare down at Freddie's board. It doesn't feel right. I try to tell myself it's just a regular board. But, all I can think about is that it belongs to Freddie. It wants me to lose.

I snap the tail and slide my front foot forward. I'm in the air.

"That's an ollie," I hear Charlie Parker Drysdale yell.

I don't get the best height but the bet wasn't about that. It was about not bailing.

I land.

BAM.

I move right into kickflip. Skateboarding is supposed to be fun, but, right now, it just feels like a big test, one that I forgot to study for.

BAM.

I land the kickflip.

I hear cheering as I head up the ramp to do a rock to fakie.

I need to be going faster. I wish I felt better on this board. I was used to my old one, the way you get so used to knowing where things are in your bedroom you don't even have to think about where the desk chair is before you drop your backpack on it. I have to think about where everything is now.

Without even knowing how I got there, my mind is thinking about missing my bedroom. And then it starts thinking about my broken board. And then about how I'll probably lose my shoes and never be able to own skate shoes or a skateboard again.

I stop at the bottom of the ramp.

The music stops too.

"Ohhhh," I hear.

"Did she bail? I knew it," shouts Freddie.

"She didn't bail," says Jake. "Still on her board."

"Whose side are you on?" asks Freddie.

"You made the rules, dude. Only one. If you bail, you lose. I'm just saying, she didn't bail."

"She will," I hear Freddie shout.

I shake my head to try and make myself stop thinking and then I ride back in the direction I just came from.

"Just get it over with," I tell myself.

I push off and skate toward the top of the ramp. On the way up, my mind starts showing me pictures of things I want to forget.

My broken board.

Saying good-bye to Vera.

I am at the top of the ramp and I hear a familiar voice calling to Freddie. I pop the front of my board over the coping.

"Stop," I tell my thoughts. "Go away."

Then I pop the board back up and over the coping again. I'm on my way back down fakie.

I head straight for the ledge.

"Sibby!" I hear Jake's voice.

You should have told that bully to back off, I say like I'm talking to Dad. *Why didn't you at least try?*

"You can stop," Jake shouts.

No way. If I stop, I lose, I tell myself and I keep going.

I hear Hannah yelling something, but the music just got loud again, and I can't hear what she's saying.

I get ready. I'm in the air.

I land my board on the ledge, but my back foot starts to slide just like before.

No other choice.

I bail.

Board flies behind me. I go down. Hard. On the ground. On my backside.

Another.

Total.

Slam.

I bailed, I tell myself as I am lying on the ground. *Again. What's happening? When did I go from being Skateboard Sibby to just Sibby?*

I lie flat out on the cement with my arms and legs spread out like you do when you're trying to make a snow angel. I hear people yelling, but I'm not sure what they're saying. The clouds are moving and that makes me feel dizzy. But then I no longer see the clouds. I see four eyes staring down at me.

"It's okay," shouts Esther. "No blood."

"And nothing broken," says Hannah. She's looking all over my body. "At least I don't think there is. No bones sticking out anyway."

Then Charlie Parker Drysdale's eyes appear.

"Whoa," he says.

"Good thing it didn't count," says Hannah.

"You better practice if you want to beat Freddie," says Esther.

"Not with this board," says Jake and now eight eyes are looking at me.

"What are you talking about?" I say and I stand up. "What do you mean, it didn't count?"

Jake is holding Freddie's board by the nose in one hand. He has his other hand out waiting for me to take off the helmet and pads.

"Where's Freddie?" I look around, but there's no sign of him.

"Had to go," says Jake. "I'll give him his stuff."

"Go?" I pass him the helmet and pads. "Where? Why?"

"Had to call it off just as you landed on the ledge," says Jake. "Just did."

"You heard him," Hannah says. She's standing in front of me winking. "Freddie called it off."

"Huh?" I say.

"You were about to tie the competition," she says, "but then Freddie had to leave so it doesn't count." She's looking at me and nodding like she wants me to nod too.

I'm confused, but I nod.

"Sorry I made you bail when we were shouting at you," says Jake. "Tomorrow. Same time and place," he says and walks away carrying Freddie's board and equipment.

"Tomorrow," says Hannah.

"I'm going to get my scooter," says Esther and she starts walking toward the bicycle rack.

"I'll come with you," says Charlie Parker Drysdale. "Sibby?" he adds.

"I'll catch up," I say. But then I wait for him to walk away before asking Hannah, "They think I bailed on purpose? Because everyone was yelling at me?"

"Exactly," she says.

"But," I say, "that's not—"

"I have to go," says Hannah, "or I'll be late for debate practice. I know you bailed. And I know it wasn't on purpose, but don't admit it, okay? I'll tell you more later," she says and starts to run back to the school.

"But," I yell after her, "how did *you* know what really happened?"

"I'll tell you later," she yells back.

Guess Hannah really does know everything.

CHAPTER 11
Time for Talking

Nan puts pumpkin-chocolate muffins and lemonade on the kitchen table. Esther is telling her all about what happened at school today.

"…and then he left," says Esther.

"That sounds like a very busy first day," says Nan.

"They're doing it again tomorrow," says Esther. "Hey, we could come over again after school and tell you what happens."

"It's so nice to have kids around this table again," says Nan. "You can come over anytime you want." And then she looks at me and adds, "As long as it's okay with Sibby."

It's not.

But Esther and Nan are both looking at me like they want me to say it's okay. I stuff muffin inside my mouth and then point at it because I can't talk with a mouth full of food.

Esther looks at me and points to her bottom lip. "Piece of chocolate right there."

Charlie Parker Drysdale passes me a napkin.

I shake my head to tell him no, and then I lick the chocolate off my lip.

"Now, I'm going to leave you three to eat your muffins," says Nan. "Pops and I will be going for a walk soon, so I have to change clothes."

"Okay," I say, but I don't get why she can't walk in the clothes she has on. She's wearing jeans and a long-sleeve shirt with yellow and white stripes.

"Your nan is so cool," says Esther. "My grandparents live in Vancouver. I'd totally love it if they were in Halifax and made muffins after school. I'd never leave."

I decide not to tell her about the sour milk.

"I still don't get why Freddie left," I say.

"It's like we told you," says Esther. "It started right around that rock fake thing."

"Rock to fakie," I say.

"Yeah that," says Esther. "My *Vogue* magazine has a whole section on skateboarding since it's in the Olympics now. I didn't read much about the jumps, just the clothes."

"They're called tricks," says Charlie Parker Drysdale, but he says it just before he takes another drink of lemonade so it makes his voice sound deep when he talks into the glass.

"Tell me again," I say. "Ms. Anderson just called his name and he ran?"

"Yep," says Esther, "and then he told Jake to call it off and you'd go again tomorrow. You barely started that last trick. The slide one. And he was gone."

"Backside bluntslide," I say. "So, then he didn't see me…" I am about to say "bail" but I remember what Hannah said and I say, "bail on purpose?"

"Nope," says Charlie Parker Drysdale, "but Jake kept videoing it with his phone."

"He did?" I say.

"He's always taking skateboarding videos," says Esther. "Hey, why aren't you finishing your muffin?"

"I dunno. I guess thinking about losing my shoes makes me not hungry," I say.

"Why are you thinking that?" asks Charlie Parker Drysdale. "This morning, you sure seemed like you thought you could win. What happened?"

I don't know how to answer Charlie Parker Drysdale. All I know is I feel different.

"If you lose, just get a new pair," says Esther. Then her eyes get big and she's smiling. "Hey, I'll go with you. I've never shopped for skateboard clothes and shoes before. You could come over to my place first, and we could plan out an entire shopping spree. We could even call it Skateboard—"

"I won these," I interrupt her. "And new ones are expensive. And I don't like sprees or any kind of clothes shopping."

"Oops, sorry," says Esther. "Forgot about your parents not having jobs."

My face feels hot. I don't like how Esther keeps reminding me about things I don't want to think about.

"Here," says Charlie Parker Drysdale before I can answer Esther, "I found videos of Freddie at the new park. Look."

He turns up the volume.

I hear Freddie's voice in the video say, "I'm gonna boardslide that five-stair hubba." I look away.

"I'm done," I say. "I can't watch Freddie skateboard anymore."

I think about Dad. Maybe he did stand up to that bully but then, like me, ended up thinking he couldn't do the thing he was always good at anymore. Maybe that's why he quit.

"So can you do those things, too?" Charlie Parker Drysdale says. "I mean, won't you have to do all new tricks tomorrow?"

The old me would have said, "Sure, I can do those things."

But I just say, "Um, yeah, maybe."

"Can you practice at the park in the morning before school?" asks Charlie Parker Drysdale. "I'll go with you."

"What's she going to practice with?" asks Esther. "No board, remember?"

I don't like the way Esther's voice sounds when she talks about me not having a board.

"Hey," she says. "My sister's boyfriend has three boards. He skateboards on the Commons mostly. I can ask if you could borrow one of his. Or, even better," she gets off her chair and bounces up and down, "I could ask my parents to loan me some money to buy you a board," she says. "I know you said you don't like clothes shopping, but we could totally focus on a board and maybe some accessories. Oh my gosh, accessories! I bet I could find pink shoes with white stars to go with my helmet. I love shopping for…"

"What? NO!" I shout. "Stop." I can't even get the words out to explain what an awful, terrible, stupid idea that is. *Loan money. Just because her parents have more than mine. What?*

Esther's not listening.

"You could pay me back," she says and she's waving her hands like I'll change my mind if I just listen to her more. "Maybe if your mom or dad get a job you could—"

"They *will* get jobs," I say.

"Finding a job isn't easy," says Charlie Parker Drysdale.

"Hey, if your dad isn't working next summer," Esther says, "maybe you could move in to our cottage and—"

I close my eyes and shout, "JUST STOP!"

I can't take it anymore. I don't want to talk about jobs or how Esther's parents have more money or moving again. Isn't it enough that I don't have a skateboard and now I'll probably lose my shoes? Why do bullies always win? Why can't Esther stop talking?

And then, when I open my eyes, more words start to fly out of me and now I'm the one who can't stop.

"My parents are totally going to get jobs. And when they do, I'm going back to my old school with my old friends, who have regular-colored hair and eat regular lunches and wear regular shoes and who know how to skateboard. This school sucks and so does living here."

"Sibby," says Charlie Parker Drysdale. He looks like he's never even seen anyone yell before. "Esther didn't mean—"

"And what would *you* know?" I say. "About any of it—other than what you blab to pretty much *anyone* who'll listen. Seriously, what is *that* about?"

Esther looks really upset. She looks like I just told her she can never, ever shop again. She walks toward the back door.

"Wait for me," says Charlie Parker Drysdale to Esther.

As he's going out the door he says, "Sure seems like Freddie isn't the only one who changed over the summer."

I can't think of one single thing to say. I keep opening my mouth hoping new words, ones that make sense, will fall out before the door shuts behind Esther and Charlie Parker Drysdale, but nothing does.

I take a deep breath.

"I am nothing like Freddie," I whisper after they leave.

I hear a weird swishing sound from behind me and then I see Pops.

"Let's talk," he says.

CHAPTER 12
Changes are Hard

Nan and Pops are dressed in matching tracksuits that swish when they move. I like to think Nan and Pops are cool, but this? This is full on *not* cool. Nan's jacket is red with a thick black stripe around each arm. The pants are all red. Pops' jacket is black with a thick red strip around each arm and the pants are all black. Pops stops swishing when we get to the living room. And then he swishes again when he sits down.

Nan swishes when she taps the space on the sofa beside her.

I sit.

"What's going on?" she asks.

I shrug.

"No shrugging," says Nan. "Shrugging is like saying 'I give up' and I've never known you to do that. Land sakes, I've seen you doing the same thing on your skateboard over and over again, trying to get it right. No, you are not a quitter. So, no shrugging, please."

"It's just that...I liked how it was," I say.

"Changes are hard," says Nan. "Even good changes take time to get used to. But you know what helps?"

"No. What?" I ask.

"Giving new things a chance. There's always a way forward, Sibby, even if it feels like you're going backward in order to get there."

"I miss Vera," I say, and I tell Nan and Pops all about Charlie Parker Drysdale and Esther's no-laces shoes and their weird lunches. And about how they kept talking about Freddie being such a great skateboarder, which made me feel like I wasn't.

"Being friends with people who aren't exactly the same as you is a good thing," says Nan. "It's how we learn to do and try new things—and their lunches sound delicious, like something maybe we could even try."

"Not the tofurkey," says Pops. "It's enough that I'm walking every day *and* that I don't use salt anymore, even though I'm a Maritimer. Maritimers need to eat extra salt. It's our connection to the sea."

"George," says Nan. "That's just ridiculous."

"It's a good theory," says Pops. "You have to admit that."

"No, I don't," says Nan. "And, from now on, Sibby's

lunches go in a lunch bag not a compost bag," she says. "Honestly."

"We all have new things to get used to," says Pops, "like making sure your cereal milk isn't outta date. Sorry about that, kiddo. Been a long, long time since I had an eleven-year-old in the house, but you know what?" Pops swishes as he leans forward in his chair.

"What?" I ask.

"Having you here is one change I'm sure glad for," says Pops. He leans back in his chair. *Swish.*

"Sibby," says Nan. "I know you're having a tough time, but Esther and Charlie have a right to be who they are just like you do. They get to like what they like and talk about what they like to talk about. Honey, you can't just yell at people when you disagree."

"They're just...they're just always doing the wrong thing," I insist.

"You didn't have to eat lunch alone on your first day, or walk to school alone," says Nan. "And it sounds like Hannah sure tried to help at the skateboard park. Everyone helps the best way they know how."

"Doesn't mean anyone has a right to push you around though," adds Pops. "Good for you for standing up to Freddie. And you can out-skateboard him. Maybe not so smart to bet your shoes on it, but you can beat him."

"I'm not so sure," I say.

"There's a secret to winning, you know," says Pops. "I bet all the best skateboarders know it."

"What?" I ask.

"It's up here." Pops points to his head. "You start doubting," he says, "you start losing."

"But I don't want to lose my shoes," I say. "And Freddie is really good. You should have seen him."

"Two rules," says Pops. "Ready?"

"I'm not so good with rules," I say. "But okay, ready."

"First, don't think about what someone else can do. Second, don't think about what you'll lose," says Pops. "Just think about riding your skateboard. Hey," he says, "that reminds me. I didn't see your skateboard when we unpacked the car."

"Yeah, um, that's because I don't have it," I say.

"*You* left your skateboard behind?" says Pops. "Now that doesn't make one bit of sense."

"It's okay," says Nan. "We'll remind your parents to bring it when they come."

"They can't," I say. "I broke it."

"What?" says Pops.

"How?" asks Nan. "Oh, Sibby."

"Cracked the deck," I say. "I tried to patch it with glue and Popsicle sticks but…whatever…it didn't work so well. I can't ask for a new one, not even for Christmas."

Pop's voice sure sounds froggy when he says, "I got it," after the doorbell rings. He swishes away.

Nan just keeps hugging me and telling me not to give up the thing I love to do.

"Promise," she whispers.

"I promise," I tell her, but it's a promise I don't know how I can keep.

"Sibby," calls Pops from the kitchen. "You have a couple of visitors."

"That's probably Charlie and Esther," says Nan.

"Can we order that pizza they like?" I ask. "Margherita?"

But then Pops says, "It's Hannah and Jake."

CHAPTER 13
It's Me or Freddie

I offer Hannah a muffin, but not Jake. And that makes him look at me like he's confused.

"What?" I say to him.

"Um." He raises his arms out to the sides. "Really?"

"Sibby," says Hannah, "Jake's here because he's trying to help."

"Why?" I ask, and I fold my arms. "What's the catch?"

"Give him a muffin," Hannah says under her breath.

"No catch," says Jake. And then he says, "Thanks," when I pass him exactly *one* muffin. Just one because I still don't know why he's here and the last time I saw him he was totally on Freddie's side and *not* mine.

"So?" I ask again. "Why are you here?"

He takes a bite and then says, "Returning a favor."

"What favor?" I ask.

"I looked up the Jackson Jo video you told me about,"

he says. "She posted it right when my sister, Mom, and I were in the middle of one of our moves."

"One of? How many times have you moved?" I ask.

"Lost count. We move because of my mom's job," he says. "But you were right. Jackson Jo says go regular not slo-mo. I'm going to send it regular. So, thanks and here," he says and passes me his phone. "I got the whole competition with you and Freddie on video. Hannah says there's something you need to see."

"What?" I look at Hannah. "I was there. I already know what happened."

"Just watch the video, Sibby," says Hannah.

I press play and watch me doing an ollie and then a kickflip. I hear the music, but the video just shows me skateboarding. Jake zoomed in and out just before and during each trick. I see me getting ready to go up the ramp and I hear things I couldn't before because the music was so loud. I hear Esther's voice.

"I know about ollies," she says. "I read about them."

"Really?" says Charlie Parker Drysdale.

"Yeah, skateboarding is in *Vogue*," she says.

"In vogue?" asks Hannah. "Do you mean like in the magazine?"

"Yeah," says Esther. "I read them all cover to cover. The cottage can get a little boring when you're alone."

101

"I know about ollies because of Sibby," says Charlie Parker Drysdale. "She's been skateboarding as long as I've known her. She's really good."

"Good as Freddie?" asks Esther. But then she answers the question at the same time as Charlie Parker Drysdale.

"I bet she is," says Esther when Charlie Parker Drysdale says, "Totally."

Hearing that makes me feel bad. Sort of. I mean why couldn't they say that to me instead of when I couldn't hear them talking?

I let the video play. It shows me stopping and then heading up the ramp to do a rock to fakie.

Next, I see me skating toward the ledge and then, as I'm about to do a backside bluntslide, I hear Jake's voice telling Freddie, "Text me. I'll get your stuff." And then he starts yelling at me to stop.

"I don't want to watch what comes next," I say, and I press pause.

Hannah takes the phone.

"Don't you want to know how I knew what really happened?" she asks. And then she presses play.

"Knew what?" asks Jake. "What do you mean what really happened?"

"We already agreed to a redo," says Hannah. "So, I guess it doesn't matter if you know."

"Know what?" He swallows the last bite of muffin.

"I didn't bail on the backside bluntslide because you were yelling at me," I say as I'm looking down at the video. "I bailed because my back foot started to—"

"What? You mean Freddie would've won?"

"He left," says Hannah. "He quit. You can't win if you quit before a competition is over."

"He had to," says Jake.

I stop listening to them because of what I see in the video. I press pause, rewind, and then play. And then I do it again.

I see it now.

I see how Hannah knew.

I pause, rewind, and watch it again. I'm on the ledge. My arms are out to the sides. My back foot is down too far on my board just before I bailed. But my foot isn't the problem. I mean it is, but it's not. The real problem is right there on my face. I have *that* look.

It's the same look Dad had when we sold our tent and when he was staring at the For Sale sign with the word *SOLD* slapped over it. It's like the look Ms. Anderson had when she did a mouth smile without her eyes smiling. It's weird because *that look* isn't about what's there but about something that's missing.

"My face," I say, and I stare at it even closer.

"Your face?" Jake takes the phone and looks at the video again.

All this time, I thought I could hide my insides. But, just like Dad's, they were right there all over my face telling everyone what I was really feeling.

"My debate coach," starts Hannah, "says faces can't lie. If you believe you can't win, it'll show. It sure showed, Sibby. Seriously, you looked like you believed you were going to lose before you even started that last trick."

I think about Pops. "I started doubting," I say. And then I think about Dad. "Just like he did."

"Who?" says Hannah.

"My dad," I say. "He was bullied."

"He was?" says Hannah.

But then Jake says, "Hold up, I don't get it."

"Have you ever been bullied?" I ask.

"Don't think so," says Jake.

"You'd know," I say. "What are you gonna do with the video?" I ask, and I hold his phone in the air.

"I showed it to you," he says, "and I'm showing it to Freddie too. I mean, the way I see it, you saw him skate, so he should see you. Hey...um...can I use your bathroom? And maybe have another one of those when I come back?" He nods in the direction of the basket of muffins now sitting on the counter.

"Upstairs." I point to the hallway behind me. "Stairs are back there. And, yeah, I guess you can have another one."

And then he walks past me and out into the hall.

I'm still holding his phone.

"Let's see it again," says Hannah. "My coach says watching yourself is the best way to get better, even though I really don't like how I look on camera. Which one was it? There."

She presses play but she's across the kitchen table from me so she does it looking at the phone upside down.

This time we're hearing different noises from before. Different as in barely anything. Just the distant sound of a skateboard on pavement.

"That's weird," I say.

Hannah takes the phone.

"Why aren't we hearing the music at least?" I ask.

"Looks like it's a different video," says Hannah. "Hey, that's not the skatepark. That's—"

And then we hear banging sounds, like a skateboard crashing into the basement door of the school.

I grab the phone. "That's the back of the school. So, there *was* a snake. I knew it. He was…oh, gross…he was spying on me? Through the trees."

"What?" says Hannah. "No. Jake wouldn't—"

"I knew it wasn't just Georgie the dog," I say.

"Oh, my gosh. This is…wow…I mean…super creepy," says Hannah.

"What a jerk-face. I mean he's here being all nice

making like he's doing me a favor, but he was spying on me." And then I start walking toward the stairs.

"Where are you going?" says Hannah. "You can't bust in on him in the bathroom."

"Gross," we both say at the same time.

"Hold on," she says. "We have to think."

"About what?" I say. "That…that stalker is using Nan and Pops' bathroom. What's wrong with him? He's no better than jerk-face Freddie!"

"I don't get him," says Hannah. "I mean he really seemed like he was trying to help. Why would he—"

"Trying to help Freddie you mean," I say. "That's why he's sending him the video of me at the skatepark today. Freddie will take one look and know I didn't bail because Jake was yelling at me. He'll know I bailed because I couldn't make the trick. And seeing that will make Freddie feel real confident. When you feel confident, you sure don't make *that* face." I point to the phone.

We hear Jake's voice upstairs and a distant swishing sound.

"He's coming," says Hannah.

"No, he's talking to one of my grandparents," I say.

I look at the video of me skateboarding in the back-yard of the school and fast-forward until the spot where I bailed comes up.

"What are you doing?" asks Hannah.

"Deleting," I say.

"What? You can't," says Hannah. "Jake said he's sending Freddie the video from the skatepark. Maybe he's not planning on sending the one in the backyard of the school."

"Or maybe he is," I say. "Then Freddie will see that I bailed on the same trick twice in one day. We can't trust Jake. I mean you're talking about the same guy that spied on me from behind some trees. That's just creepy."

"So you're going to delete his video?"

"No. I'm only deleting the part where I bailed," I say. "And I'm sending it to Freddie. Maybe if he thinks I made the trick he won't want to do it again tomorrow."

"Oh, no," says Hannah. "That sounds like a terrible idea."

I press the Share button and tap the Message icon.

"Sibby, think this through."

"You're right," I say. "The message has to explain why the video ends when I'm in mid-air."

"Not what I meant," says Hannah.

I type, "Saw her land. Someone came. Couldn't keep shooting. She's no poser. Real deal." I don't know Freddie's number so I type his name until it appears in the field marked "To."

Hannah is telling me about all the things that make what I am about to do a really bad move.

"...and what if Freddie texts Jake back? Then he'll know it was us," she argues.

I ignore everything Hannah is saying until she asks, "Sibby. Is this really *you?*"

I look at Hannah. "I'm...I don't know."

Maybe sending this means I'm as bad as Freddie is for bullying and as bad as Jake is for spying. Maybe I should try to be more like Vera. She'd be chill. She wouldn't do this. Nan and Pops wouldn't either. I shouldn't. My thumb is closer to the button that will delete the text message than it is to the one that will send it.

We hear Jake coming down the stairs.

And then my brain starts picturing Freddie being a bully. And I start remembering all the trouble that bullies cause.

I can't stand that this bully—my bully—might win. I can't stand that he'll get more confidence watching me lose mine.

"Sibby?" says Hannah.

"What would you do if this was a debate you needed to win?" I ask her. "Seriously needed to win."

"I...um..." Hannah stutters. "I..."

It's me or Freddie, I tell myself.

"I wouldn't," she says just as I press Send.

"Too late," I say.

"Your grandparents sure are nice," says Jake and then he reaches for another muffin before sitting down again.

Hannah and I are just staring at him.

"What?" he says.

CHAPTER 14
Scary Stuff

On our way to school, Charlie Parker Drysdale is talking about how he's still mad at me, but his mothers told him he had to walk to school with me anyway and blah, blah, blah. He is wearing a yellow sweater-vest over a yellow T-shirt. He sure is bright, like the sun with arms and legs.

"I mean, yeah, I tell stuff," he says. His hands are waving in front of him as he talks, "But it just comes out. It's how I think. Mom and Mama both say some people think best by talking. I mean maybe you don't, but I do, so stuff comes out."

I can't listen anymore. I keep thinking about Jake's phone and how I shouldn't have sent the video to Freddie. I wish I could take it all back. All sorts of thoughts are running around in my head.

What if Jake and Freddie talked last night?

What if Jake told Freddie all about how I bailed in the

backyard and Freddie gets more confidence even without seeing the video?

What if Nan and Pops find out?

What if Vera finds out I broke my one rule: Skateboarders help each other.

What if deleting parts of videos and sending fake texts is who I am now?

But then I start thinking about Jake spying on me and I get mad all over again. I mean he seemed so nice coming over last night saying he was trying to help.

Some help.

When we walk into the classroom, I put my helmet on the shelf beside Esther's. Next, I hang my backpack on a hook. Knee and elbow pads are inside. Instead of three skateboards, today there are only two. The ghost board and another that is either Freddie's or Jake's. Their boards look exactly the same. I glance around the room. I don't see Freddie but I see Jake sitting at his desk talking to Hannah. I can only see the sides of their heads. Jake looks the same as always and Hannah is smiling. And that can only mean one thing.

Jake doesn't know what I did, so neither does Freddie.

At least I hope that's what it means.

Charlie Parker Drysdale goes to his desk and starts talking to Esther.

Hannah gives me a thumbs up as I get closer to her

111

and Jake. When I sit down she says, "Jake and I were just talking about how he sent the video of Freddie to Jackson Jo when he got home last night."

"Cool," I say. "You hear back?" I ask and I stare at Jake's face. I am trying to see if I can tell for sure if he knows what I did.

I totally can't.

"Not yet," he says. "But there's something we need to talk about."

Uh-oh.

He takes what looks like a big piece of paper from under the notepad sitting on his desk.

"This," he says. "I turned the part right before you bailed into a still shot and printed it. Here."

Whew!

He passes me the picture.

"I still don't get why you guys were talking about your face," he says.

And then he looks up and, before I can say anything, Jake says, "Uh-oh."

He's looking toward the front of the class, so I do too.

Mr. MacDonald is standing in front of Ms. Anderson's desk.

"Think I know why Freddie left the park so fast yesterday *and* why he didn't text last night," Jake says.

Mr. MacDonald tells us that he's filling in for Ms.

Anderson. He says that she and Freddie will be out for a few days and that we'll have a substitute teacher.

"Both of them?" asks Hannah.

I turn around and look at Jake.

"Unfortunately," says Mr. MacDonald, "I have some sad news. Freddie's grandfather passed away last night."

"He did?" says Charlie Parker Drysdale through the sounds of people saying things like "Oh, no!" and "What?"

"But," says Esther, "what does that have to do with Ms. Anderson? Why isn't she here?"

"Are they related?" I ask Jake, but I'm pretty sure I know the answer. All I have to do is think about crooked pinkies.

"Guess it'll come out sooner or later," says Jake to me. But then he starts talking to everyone in the classroom. "Ms. Anderson is Freddie's aunt. He lives with her now. He has ever since the summer when his grandpa got sick. Didn't want anyone to know, but now that his grandpa died, I guess it won't be a secret much longer."

"Wow, he really did have a worse summer than me," I say.

"Maybe that's why he's been so mean," says Hannah. "My dad says mean people are just really unhappy."

"You can't go around being a bully," I say. "Even if something really, really bad happens like…" I stop myself

113

because saying that Freddie's grandpa died makes me think about Pops dying and I do *not* want to think about that.

"Why wouldn't Freddie just tell us his grandpa was sick?" asks Esther. "*And* that Ms. Anderson is his aunt?"

"Guess he thought we'd blab," says Charlie Parker Drysdale and he looks at me.

"Or maybe he just didn't want to talk about it," I say and I look back at him.

"Did you ever think," says Charlie Parker Drysdale, "that you have way too many secrets?"

"Just 'cause I tell you something, or Nan tells your moms, doesn't mean you can go ahead and tell everyone else," I say. "How is that being a friend? And how is reminding me about seeing me fall off my board being a friend?"

"Because you always get back up," says Charlie Parker Drysdale. "But ever since you moved here, you keep looking at everything like it's all bad. Isn't anything good?"

"Okay, okay," says Mr. MacDonald. "Time to chill, or breathe, or find your happy place—call it what you will but you can't think straight when you're rattled. No one can."

"That's what my debate coach says too," says Hannah. "It's actually pretty funny. Ready? Keep calm because…the debate will carry on." Hannah is the only one who laughs.

"Look," says Mr. MacDonald. "Some things are hard to figure out and even harder to talk about. Like losing someone or something you love. Or having your parents split up. Or moving to a new town. Or joining a team when you don't know anyone. Or," he looks at me and at Charlie Parker Drysdale, "feeling like a friend has let you down or that you let them down," he says. "It can make us feel weird, even afraid. And it's really hard to talk about what makes us feel weird and afraid. And you're right," Mr. MacDonald looks back at me. "Just because Freddie's grandpa died doesn't mean he has the right to be a bully. Maybe he needs to figure out what he's so afraid of. Maybe we all do. Maybe that's the place to start."

"Can English be where we start?" says Jake. "I'd rather talk about grammar."

"Me too," says Mr. MacDonald. "I'd rather talk about grammar, or basketball, or how I made the best casserole of my life last night. But emotions are complicated and can get all twisted inside of us." He walks around to the other side of the desk and asks us to take out a piece of paper. "I have an idea," he announces. "How about you try to write down what scares you most?"

A few people groan.

"Don't worry. You don't have to show it to anyone," says Mr. MacDonald. "You can talk it out with each other or keep it to yourself forever if you like."

"Why do it if we're not going to talk about it?" asks Charlie Parker Drysdale.

I roll my eyes.

"Because not everyone thinks best by talking about it, Charlie," says Mr. MacDonald. "And it's important to admit what scares you, if only to yourself. To say 'Yeah, that scares me, but I'm not gonna let being afraid get in my way.'"

Mr. MacDonald takes out a piece of paper and sits at his desk. "I'll do it too," he says and starts writing.

I take out a piece of paper and a pencil. I don't know what to write. Then I look over at Charlie Parker Drysdale. He's writing down a ton of things.

Esther writes something. Stops. And then starts writing again. I turn around. Jake is staring straight ahead.

"What?" he says. "I'm done."

I look down at his paper.

"Quit it," he says.

I turn back around. I still don't know what to write, so I just start drawing a skateboard. Then I feel someone looking over my shoulder.

"Seriously?" says Charlie Parker Drysdale and he's pointing at my drawing, "You're not doing it?"

"What the...hey!" I lift my head to see him looking at my paper. "Stop looking." I cover my paper.

"You looked at Jake's," he says and then he sits down in his seat and lifts his paper. "Here," he says. "I don't care if you see my list."

"Dude," says Jake. "You have a list?"

"Things going okay?" asks Mr. MacDonald.

"Did you want us to make a list or just name one thing?" asks Charlie Parker Drysdale.

"Whatever applies," says Mr. MacDonald. "And I encourage you to talk to each other about what you've written, but let's keep it to a whisper, so those who aren't finished won't be disturbed."

"Sorry," says Charlie Parker Drysdale. And then he pulls his desk closer to mine and Jake's and says, "Don't you have a list?"

"No," says Jake quietly. "Just one thing."

"Being new?" I ask Jake.

"Nope," he says. "When you move as much as I have you get used to being new and making friends. Keeping 'em is the hard part. So that's what I wrote down."

"Is that why you just go along with Freddie when he starts picking on people?" asks Esther.

"Shhh," says Charlie Parker Drysdale, waving his hand to signal that Esther should come closer.

"It's not like that," says Jake.

Esther pulls her desk closer and whispers, "Seems like it's exactly like that."

"She's right. I mean you went along with him, yesterday," says Charlie Parker Drysdale.

"Sibby stood up to him," says Jake. His voice rises. He looks past me at Mr. MacDonald and then back at me and whispers, "Didn't think you needed help."

"So you helped Freddie instead," I say.

"How?" he asks.

I take the still shot he printed and hold it up. "You wanted him to know about that face," I point to the picture. "Even when you stand up to a bully, they still get inside your head, especially when you're the *only* one doing the standing up. So, that…" I point to my face in the picture, "*that's* what being bullied looks like."

"What?" says Charlie Parker Drysdale.

Esther takes the picture from my hand and examines it. Charlie Parker Drysdale does too.

"You sure don't look happy," says Esther.

"So you bailing at the park is all my fault?" says Jake.

"Not totally," says Hannah who is now kneeling between Jake's desk and Charlie Parker Drysdale's desk. "But going along with a bully only helps the bully. I mean I'm *really* sorry about Freddie's grandpa, but I don't want to spend the entire year being called Big-eyes-banana."

Hannah stands up. "Sorry, Mr. MacDonald," she says because she didn't whisper that last part.

"Thank you," he says. But he says it loud because there is a ton of whispering in the classroom now.

"And I don't want to spend the year being Esther-blue-hair," says Esther.

"Okay, okay," says Jake. "I get it."

"You sure?" I ask him, and I totally don't sound chill when I add, "Or are you just saying that?"

"What's with you?" asks Jake. "What kind of question is that?"

"I don't like being spied on," I snap.

"What are you talking about?" Esther asks.

"He secretly videoed me from behind the trees. Creep," I hiss.

"Hold on!" says Jake.

"You spied?" asks Charlie Parker Drysdale.

"Ewww," says Esther.

"Jake videoed Sibby skateboarding at lunch yesterday," says Hannah. "Without her knowing."

"Out back," I say.

Charlie Parker Drysdale has a funny look on his face.

"It's not like that," says Jake. "It's nothing."

"Sure seems like something," I tell him.

"You need to explain," says Esther, "because that sounds really bad."

"I ran home for a few minutes after I ate my lunch," says Jake. He points his thumb toward the windows. "I

119

live in that brown house on the other side of the empty lot behind the school. I wasn't sure if you were telling me the truth about Jackson Jo and slo-mo. I mean, I don't know you, right?"

"So you thought I was setting you up?" I ask.

"Maybe. I wanted to see for myself," he says, "but then I saw you skating. We couldn't find anything online of you skateboarding and Freddie was a little freaked out. I mean, he won't admit it, but he knows about the Charlottetown Invitational and, hey, you came second. That's dope. So when I saw you out there, I started videoing to show him what kind of skater you are. But, I mean, you didn't just fall, that was a slam. I ran to see if you were okay, but you went in through the basement door. When I came inside with everyone else, I saw that you were fine."

"Sounds sort of reasonable," says Esther.

"Not to me," I say. "You were spying on me to help Freddie beat me. And that's not cool. I mean you know what it's like to be new and you weren't just being a jerk-face, you were being a super jerk-face." I am getting madder and madder as I talk. "And that's why—"

"Sibby, don't," says Hannah.

"That's why I'm totally glad I deleted the part of the video where I bailed and sent it to Freddie," I blurt.

"You messed with a video I took?" shouts Jake in a loud voice. "When?"

"Shhh," says Charlie Parker Drysdale.

Hannah hangs her head. "Last night," she says. "When you were upstairs."

"Were you in on it?" he asks Hannah. "Was the whole 'hey come on over and have a muffin' thing a setup?"

"No," says Hannah. "We didn't even know about your spying until you went upstairs."

"I wasn't spying," he says.

"Jake," says Mr. MacDonald. "Voice down, please."

"Did you know Hannah and Jake were coming over last night?" Esther asks me.

"What?" I say because I don't get why she's asking me that right now. "What's the difference?"

"Did you have pizza?" asks Esther.

I ignore her and look at Jake. "And you were probably going to put it online somewhere anyway, right?"

"You really think that?" says Jake.

"Um, you were hiding in the bushes," says Charlie Parker Drysdale.

"I told you it wasn't like that!" shouts Jake.

"Okay, okay. Seems like we are well past whispering and into full-on shouting," Mr. MacDonald says. "It's one thing to have a lively discussion, but it sure doesn't sound like—"

He's saying more, but none of us can hear him because we are all yelling at each other.

Mr. MacDonald stands in front of Freddie's empty desk and shouts "HEY! STOP SHOUTING!" which, I think, is a very strange way to get people to stop shouting.

Then, when no one is shouting, he tells us he has a new idea. And when he tells us what it is, I decide I don't like Mr. MacDonald's ideas.

His new idea is this: Charlie Parker Drysdale, Hannah, Esther, Jake, and I all need to stay in the classroom—together—and eat lunch—together. And no one can leave until lunch is over. No one, except Mr. MacDonald.

CHAPTER 15
Owner of the Ghost Board

Mr. MacDonald says he needs to supervise the lunchroom so he can't stay for all of our together time.

"Aren't you at least going to tell us what you wrote about what scares you most?" asks Charlie Parker Drysdale.

"Sure," he says as he's walking toward the classroom door. "Being a good teacher."

"What?" says Jake. "Really?"

"Yeah," he says. "I like teaching. I want to do it well, but sometimes it's hard to know. And teaching isn't just about a subject, at least not to me. It's also about the hard stuff, like helping a group of friends stay friends. So, I'm hoping you'll find a way." He smiles, waves, and shuts the door behind him.

No one waves back. Charlie Parker Drysdale is drinking juice. Hannah is chomping on an apple while flipping through books from the shelf over by the windows. Esther is reading a magazine, and Jake is still talking about how I messed with his video and how Mr. MacDonald took his phone, so he can't even check to see if Jackson Jo got back to him.

"Hey," I say, "you're the one who—"

"Just quit it," says Esther. She's looking at both of us but still turning the pages in front of her. "Jake took a video of Sibby and Sibby cut part of it out. Big deal." She starts flipping the pages of her magazine really hard. "I didn't do any of that, and now I'm stuck here thanks to you." Esther looks up from her magazine at me. "And, Sibby, I still don't get what you were so mad about last night. I was only trying to help. Whatever. I'm done," she says and stands up. "I'm getting sick of reading about skateboarding, even if it is in *Vogue*." She walks toward the bookshelf but her magazine falls off her desk as she moves past it.

She looks down but then just shakes her head and walks past the magazine without picking it up.

A line on the cover says, "Interview with Jackson Jo, page 20."

"I'll get it," I say and I reach for the magazine at the same time as Charlie Parker Drysdale reaches for a piece of folded paper that fell out of the pages. He opens the paper and makes a face.

"What?" I ask.

He looks up at Esther, who is talking to Hannah, and then he passes the paper to me.

It says, "Being alone."

"Why'd you open this?" I whisper. "It's what she wrote down. It's about what she's afraid of."

Charlie Parker Drysdale rolls his eyes. "So? Why does everything have to be top secret with you?"

"Because it's private," I say.

Esther comes back and sits at her desk. She sees me holding the paper.

Jake is over at the rack where the skateboards are, and Hannah is still at the bookshelf.

"I...uh," I start. And I wish I could figure out what to say, but sometimes when I try to say stuff about feelings it all comes out wrong, even when I don't mean for it to.

As I'm thinking about what to say, Charlie Parker Drysdale keeps it simple. He tells Esther this: "You're not alone."

She smiles. Face and eyes. "Thanks, Charlie."

And that's when I decide that maybe his talking without thinking isn't awful *all* of the time.

I look at him and whisper, "That was cool."

He nods and then sits up straighter at his desk.

I decide to do what Charlie Parker Drysdale did and just say what I'm thinking. Here goes. "Esther," I say.

"What you wrote. Is that the reason you wanted to go shopping with me? And why you said we could move in to your cottage? Because you don't want to...you know...be alone?"

"Mostly," she says. "I thought it would be fun, and it's not like *my parents* spend lots of time at the cottage. It'd be nice to have people there. People I like."

"It's...well, I thought you were saying those things because my parents can't...really afford stuff," I say. "Whatever. I shouldn't have yelled." And then I look at Charlie Parker Drysdale. "At either of you. Sorry."

Esther nods.

"My moms say you're probably upset about moving," says Charlie Parker Drysdale.

"Is it really that bad here?" asks Esther.

"No," I answer. "It's not really about moving. It's... it's...just...everything's changed."

"It gets easier," says Jake. He and Hannah are now back in their seats. "We lived up north in Iqaluit, and I mean I thought I'd never get used to it getting dark right after lunch during the winter. But it was kinda cool. Glad I lived there now. You should see my northern lights videos."

"Can you bring them?" asks Charlie Parker Drysdale.

"Sure," says Jake. "When?"

"How about tonight?" I say, which kinda surprises me. It's weird to be surprised by something you hear yourself say, but I totally am. And then I surprise myself even more when I look at Esther and Charlie Parker Drysdale and say, "We could even have pizza Margherita. I mean I was totally going to invite you for some last night."

"You were?" asks Esther.

"Yeah, I asked Nan if it was okay, but then it was Hannah and Jake at the door when I thought it was you and Charlie Parker Drysdale coming back," I explain.

"Pizza sure would have been better than veggie casserole with a side of herbed tofu," says Charlie Parker Drysdale.

"So? Tonight?" I ask.

"I'll come," says Esther before I barely have the words out.

"Me too," says Charlie Parker Drysdale.

"And me," says Hannah.

"Um, didn't you just call me a spy and admit to deleting part of one of my videos?" says Jake. "And now you're asking me over? For pizza?"

"I'm sorry about all of that. Sort of. Mostly," I say, "but not all the way sorry. I mean videoing me without telling me? Pretty sketchy."

"I swear I didn't think of it like that," says Jake. "It's just, Freddie has been dealing with his grandpa being sick and I was trying to help. If I had thought of it like you just said, I never would've done it."

"Okay then," I tell him. "I'm all the way sorry. One hundred percent. It's just that I believed you last night when you said you were trying to help. And then when I saw the video you took of me behind the school…sure seemed like you were as big a jerk as Freddie. But, you're not a jerk. And I won't mess with any of your videos ever again."

Jake just looks at me like he's not sure what to say.

"I swear," I add.

I lift my fist.

Jake does too.

We bump.

"See that?" Charlie Parker Drysdale is pointing at our fist bump. "That's what happens when you talk about things."

I stare at him. I'm not ready to agree, but it's possible—a tiny bit possible—that maybe he's right about that. This one time.

"I can't do pizza tonight though," says Jake. "After I hit the park and my mom gets home from work, I need to go see Freddie."

I feel happy that I won't have to skateboard against Freddie today but sad about the reason.

"Hey," says Charlie Parker Drysdale. "There's just one thing that doesn't make sense."

"What?" I ask.

"It's about what you said before. You know, when you were talking about Jake and the video."

"Yeah?" I ask.

"How did you go skateboarding at lunch yesterday?" he asks. "You broke yours. That's why you had to trick Freddie into lending his. Right?"

"You broke your board?" says Jake. "When?"

"Before I moved here," I say.

"Whoa," says Jake. "So you don't have a board anymore? That's hard-core," he says. But then he looks confused. "But, um, then what about what Charlie said? Where'd you get the board you were riding? I didn't see you with one yesterday, but I figured one of the guys from the park lent you one, and you went out back to skate so Freddie'd leave you alone."

"Nope," I say, and I look at Hannah. "I sort of borrowed one. From over there," I point to the shelf. "There's a really cool ghost board that's been just sitting there. Pretty sure someone left it behind or something."

Jake jumps up and runs over to the shelf.

"Where'd you get a helmet and pads and stuff?" Charlie Parker Drysdale asks. "You didn't have those with you yesterday either."

"I kind of didn't wear any," I say.

"Seriously?" says Charlie Parker Drysdale.

"You should have at least had a helmet, Sibby," says Esther.

"Wow," says Hannah. "I'd rather break anything other than my brain."

Jake is holding the skateboard I used yesterday and turning it over and over like he's trying to make sure there aren't any scratches on it.

"Bad call, Sibby," he says. "Very bad."

"I know," I say. "I shouldn't have tried a backside bluntslide without a helmet. And I have to get a couple more scuffs out of the board, but I can do that with—"

"No. It's not only that," says Jake. And he says it in a panicky-sounding voice. "You can't use this board, like *ever* again. Got it?"

And now his face is looking panicked too. And when I put his panicky-sounding voice and his panicked-looking face together in my brain, something tells me he's going to say that the board I borrowed is—

"It's Freddie's board," says Jake.

"Uh-oh," says Charlie Parker Drysdale and he puts his hands up against his cheeks.

"No way," says Esther.

"Why did he leave it there?" asks Hannah.

"His grandpa gave it to him to use at the new park," says Jake.

"Oh, my gosh," Hannah says, and now she brings her hands to her cheeks.

"And he *left* it there?" I point to the shelf. "That doesn't make sense. Are you sure?"

"Yeah, I'm sure. No one ever touches our boards," says Jake. "Freddie and I took this one to the park the night before school started. But then Freddie decided he couldn't skate with it. He said he was going to wait until his grandpa got better and could come watch him. Ms. Anderson was inside getting things ready for school, so he left it here and we went back to the park."

"How come he didn't say anything to Sibby about not having a board when he dared her to skateboard against him yesterday?" asks Charlie Parker Drysdale. "She didn't have one with her."

"I doubt he noticed," says Jake. "All he talked about was how she came back at him and kept calling him out. He wasn't expecting any of that. Probably too surprised to think about it. I mean we didn't even know she was in our class until she walked in. And no one else in our class skateboards or even looks at these boards. All I know is that the dude's gonna go *CRAZY* if he finds out she used *this* board."

"So don't tell," says Charlie Parker Drysdale, and

that makes us all look at him, because it's funny to hear Charlie Parker Drysdale talk about keeping a secret.

"What?" he says as we are all staring at him. He points to the shelf. "I know I'm not supposed to tell anyone about *that*, so I won't." He pulls his fingers across his lips like he's closing a zipper.

"Uh-oh," says Hannah.

"What?" I say.

Then Jake looks up from the board like he's thinking the same thing Hannah's thinking. His mouth is open.

"What?" I ask again.

"Didn't you say you sent—" starts Jake.

"Ohmygoshthevideo," says Hannah.

"Uh-oh," I say.

Mr. MacDonald comes back in the room.

"So," he asks with a smile, "everyone feeling better?"

CHAPTER 16
Skaters Know Their Boards

I t is really hard to sit through computer lab *and* music class when your insides feel like they are thrashing around like ocean waves in the middle of a hurricane. Nothing helps. Not even bouncing your legs up and down so much they actually hurt a little. And my legs aren't all that's bouncing. The thoughts in my head are too. It's like a million basketballs dropped on a court from the sky and they're bouncing so fast and so loud I can't think straight.

Why didn't I just listen to Vera? Stay chill. Avoid trouble. Was that really so hard? Instead, this is what I did: I found trouble, got mad, and called Freddie names. Then I used his skateboard, the one his grandpa gave him. And the whole time, I was the opposite of chill.

At least I got the last of the scuff marks out of the board, thanks to Mr. MacDonald letting me and Hannah go downstairs to borrow the belt-sander cleaner from her father again. Now the board looks like it did before I used it.

Jake, Esther, Charlie Parker Drysdale, and Hannah are all talking at the same time on our way to the skatepark.

Hannah is saying we need a new plan in case Freddie figures out it was his board I used. Jake just keeps saying "A skater knows his board." Esther thinks we should go buy Freddie a new one. Charlie Parker Drysdale says he can't decide if keeping a secret really is best and that maybe we should just tell Freddie the truth and then all talk about it.

"Um…no," I say to that last part.

"Here," says Jake. He passes me his board.

"What?" I ask as I take it.

"You look rattled," he says. "It's like Mr. MacDonald says, you can't think when you're rattled. Just take it. Do a few runs."

I don't like that I can't hide my insides, but it's nice to know I can trust Jake to help me make them calm again.

"Over here," says Hannah. "There's shade from the sign. We'll be able to see the video better in the shade. Maybe you can't tell what the board actually looks like. Maybe all you can see is that Sibby's just riding some unknown board."

"I better come too," I tell Jake.

"Trust me," he says. "We'll watch the video and then

134

tell you if you can see that the board is Freddie's. I mean, hey, maybe I didn't zoom in close enough, right? Maybe?"

"Maybe," I nod and take his board. "Thanks," I say just before I do a drop in. Hearing the sound of the wheels on the cement and feeling the air against my face help my thoughts stop bouncing all over the inside of my brain.

Jake, Hannah, Esther, and Charlie Parker Drysdale are all standing under the rules sign staring at Jake's phone.

"Can't really see it," says Hannah.

"She's really far away," says Charlie Parker Drysdale.

"Keep watching," says Jake. "I'm telling you, if it's even close to being in view, Freddie will know his board. We have to be sure it's not in any of the frames."

There's a rainbow ahead. Not in the sky, in the middle of the park. A skatepark rainbow is cement in the shape of an arc. This one's covering a gap filled with rocks.

Kickflip over the gap, I tell myself right before I do it.

BAM.

I land and ride back toward the gap to do it again. It's not only the sound of the landing that makes me feel better. I mean I love that sound, but there is something else I love.

It's being in the air and having a skateboard underneath me. Even though I'm not touching it, I know it's there. It's waiting for me.

BAM.

Together, the board and I land and then we glide forward. I look up at my new friends as I skate. They're all still staring at that video, and I think about how dope it is that they make me feel the same way this board does. Like it's okay to land.

I head toward the five-stair hubba. I'm going to 50 the whole thing.

I ollie onto the hubba and start to slide, but I shift my weight and I know I'm headed for a slam.

I bail and land on my backside.

I let my helmet touch the cement as I stare back at that hubba. And then I hear a familiar voice inside my head. But this time it's not Vera's, it's Charlie Parker Drysdale's voice from when we were arguing in the classroom. "Because you always get back up," he had said.

So that's what I do. I get back up, but instead of going back to the hubba, I decide to 50 the rainbow. It's easier than doing that on a five-stair hubba.

I ollie and land at the arch of the rainbow and then 50 the half. Without thinking about it, I skate back to the hubba. I ollie onto it and start to slide. I slide until I'm almost at the end. Pop out and *BAM*.

It worked. Going back to the rainbow helped me conquer the hubba. And now I know what Nan meant when she said, "There's always a way forward, even if it feels like you're going backward in order to get there."

I'm smiling as I skate away from the hubba.

"You always get back up." I hear Charlie Parker Drysdale's voice again, but this time it's not in my head. He's yelling it from the top of the park near the rules sign. I raise my arm in the air and wave.

"SUPER DOPE," I hear Jake yell and then I see all of them running toward me.

"Hey, it's okay," says Esther as she gets closer. She's on her scooter.

"Yeah, you totally can't see the board," says Hannah. "We watched it over and over."

I am feeling the most chill I have felt all day. "That's so good," I say, "because I was worried about the stars on the deck hitting the sunlight. I mean if you get the right angle you could—"

"HEY," shouts a familiar voice. "UP HERE."

"Uh-oh," I say.

Jake and Charlie Parker Drysdale are on one side of me and Esther and Hannah are on the other. Freddie is standing at the top of the park yelling down at me.

"YOU USED IT? BEFORE I DID?"

"This is not good," says Esther.

"A skater always knows their board," says Jake. "Even if it's barely in view."

CHAPTER 17
Sudden Death

Freddie and I are now face-to-face near the rules sign. He's yelling so loud that everyone who was skateboarding is standing around watching the fireworks.

Jake keeps saying, "Dude. Easy," but Freddie's not listening. He's not listening to anything. He's not even trying. He's holding the same board he always uses with one hand and waving his other hand around as he yells.

There's only one way I can think of to get him to stop screaming. I reach down and grab his board.

"*What the...*" Freddie's eyes are gigantic. He lunges for the board, but I pull it out of reach.

"SHUT UP!" I shout. And then in a regular voice I say, "For a minute." And then I say, "Please." Seems to me that people who are chill say please.

He looks at me, and then the board, and then back at me. Before he can start yelling again, I start talking.

"Yeah, I took it," I tell him. "Totally didn't know it was yours. Didn't know your grandpa gave it to you. A BIG mistake. GINORMOUS. But, I just wanted to skate. That's all. I'm sorry. I am. I'm really sorry."

Freddie just keeps staring at me.

"Freddie, dude," says Jake. "It was a mistake. I checked the board all over and it's cool. Looks just like it did when your grandpa gave it to you."

"YOU KNEW!" Freddie shouts. Now he's staring at Jake.

"He just found out," I say.

"What's up with you?" says Freddie, still looking at Jake. "Didn't even come around last night."

"Didn't know till this morning," says Jake. "Mr. MacDonald told us."

"You sure seem chummy with this crew," Freddie points to me, Esther, Hannah, and Charlie Parker Drysdale.

"Man, come on, you know I woulda been there if I knew," says Jake.

"Whatever, dude. You wanna hang out with a bunch of losers, be my guest."

"Serious," says Jake. "This isn't cool."

Freddie starts hating all over me again. He's calling me a poser and a freak show and he's totally getting in my face. We're nose to nose. Again. I clench my fists and not because I want to feel the trucks of a skateboard, but because I am angrier than I've ever been.

"You are gonna wish you never came to this school," he says, and he's so close to me I know he had something with onions for lunch. Yuck. I hold my breath.

"Freddie," says Hannah. "Sibby said it was a mistake." Freddie doesn't move. And neither do I.

"You need to back off," I say, blowing out the air I was holding in.

"Or what?" he says.

I stare at Freddie and I totally see a jerk-face bully. But it's weird, because I see something else too. I see the answer to the question Mr. MacDonald asked us. I know what scares me most.

And it's *not* Freddie.

It's *not* a bully.

It's what's already happened.

It's all the changes.

Breaking my board. Not being able to get a new one. Feeling like I'm not a skateboarder anymore. Saying good-bye to Vera. Being so mad at Dad. Starting somewhere new. So many changes—all at once. It made me feel like I lost something. Except it wasn't just one thing. It was a whole bunch of somethings that added up to one giant something.

But it's okay. It's going to keep being okay. I can do this. I don't need to be scared anymore.

I take a deep breath and let out a whole bunch of air. My fists are no longer clenched.

Freddie's eyes are staring at me but he's not really seeing me. He's just seeing what he's lost.

"There's only one thing to do." I give Freddie back his board.

And then I lift Jake's board up beside my head.

"What are you doing?" Freddie says.

"Time to skate," I say. "Let's finish what we started."

"You want to compete again?" he asks.

"Sure," I tell him, but not because I want to beat him this time. I mean I do, but it's more about what Mr. MacDonald said. "You can't think when you're rattled."

Freddie is pretty rattled. There's no point in talking. He needs to skate.

"You ready?" I ask.

"Always," he says, and he has a really mean look on his face. "But this time, we play S.K.A.T.E."

Vera and I used to play all the time.

It goes like this: Each player does whatever trick they want. If they land it, the next person to go needs to land it too. Whoever bails, gets a letter. The first person to get S, K, A, T, and E loses.

"Let's do it," I tell him.

"Not so fast," he says. "We play my version. No more of the simple stuff any poser could do. My rules. *If* you dare."

"What are your rules?" asks Esther.

"I go first," says Freddie.

"Whatever," I say. "Fine."

"And I shout the trick just before I do it," he says. "If you land it, you take a turn in the lead. Unless one of us bails, it's back to me in the lead and so on. Got it?"

"Got it." I nod.

"There's more," Freddie continues. "First one to bail on *any* trick gets all the letters at once. Sudden death."

Freddie puts his helmet on.

"In or out?" he says.

Even though I'm feeling more confident, Freddie's version of S.K.A.T.E. has me doubting myself again. But, I have to do it anyway. Just as I'm about to tell Freddie I'm in, I look at Esther, Hannah, and Charlie Parker Drysdale and decide the bet needs to change.

"I have new terms."

"What?" says Freddie.

What Pops said was true. Freddie doesn't have the right to bully me or my new friends because his grandpa died.

"You lose, you stop calling out Charlie Parker Drysdale about his sweater-vests *and* stop making fun of Esther's blue hair."

"Thanks, Sibby," says Esther.

"Don't get too happy," says Freddie to Esther. "She's gonna lose."

I look at Hannah. She's staring at me through those big round glasses.

"And leave Hannah and her glasses alone, too," I say.

"I still get your ugly shoes," he says.

"Then she still gets your board," says Charlie Parker Drysdale.

"You get *this* one," says Freddie and he holds up the board he always uses. "But there's one more thing."

"What?" I ask.

"When I win," he says, and he steps closer to me, "you can never, *ever* use this skatepark again." He waves his arm all around him like he's trying to make sure I know what he means by "this skatepark."

"What!?" says Hannah. "That's nuts."

"No way," says Esther.

"Don't do it, Sibby," says Charlie Parker Drysdale.

"Freddie," says Jake. "Come on, man."

I sure wasn't expecting that. But, I wasn't expecting to make friends either and I'm tired of being scared.

"You know what?" I put my helmet on my head. "I'll take your bet."

"Enjoy your last skate at this park," says Freddie as he's dropping in. I jump on Jake's board and follow Freddie.

He's headed toward the wooden ledge I bailed off during yesterday's competition. I'm pretty sure he's going to try another backside bluntslide, so I get ready.

He's riding on an angle toward the ledge. Someone turned up the music, and it's really loud.

Freddie ollies and yells, "Frontside nosegrind!"

Ugh, I have to change the picture in my head. It's okay though. Doing a frontside nosegrind has always come easy for me. I'm not on a good angle, but I pop up on the ledge. My front foot is right where Jackson Jo says it should be: right behind the bolts on the deck.

Don't stick. Don't stick.

I come to the end of the ledge, pop the nose of my board, level out, and land.

My heart is beating really fast. Freddie sure means business, but so do I.

I push off and head toward the pyramid. I glance down at my shoes and start thinking about how it will feel to lose them to Freddie. Then I remember what Pops said: "Just think about riding your skateboard."

I'm at the pyramid. "Backside flip!" I yell. And I skate up, ollie, flip. *BAM.*

"Easy!" shouts Freddie and he follows right behind me. *BAM.* He lands. I barely have time to catch my breath when Freddie is skating into the bowl.

He is pushing really hard, but I'm right behind him.

"Frontside invert," he yells as he heads up the wall. When he gets to the top, he reaches for the coping with one hand. His body and board float into the air. He's almost completely upside down.

The people watching us are going crazy. I mean that is a serious trick. If I'm going to beat him, I can't just land the tricks he yells out. I need to make my tricks harder. I love inverts, which is why I used to practice them over and over. Sometimes I bail but *not today,* I tell myself.

I'm up the wall. I reach for the coping with my right hand and feel my body and my board leave the ground. We're basically upside down.

"*WHOAAAAAA*," I hear voices yelling. "SICK."

I bring myself and my board back down.

"GO SIBBY," I hear. "GO FREDDIE."

Everyone is going crazy yelling at us.

I ride back down the wall trying to figure out what the next trick should be. But then I see Freddie skating hard in my direction.

"Wrong way," he shouts as he passes me.

"Where are you going?" I stop quick. "It's my turn to be in the lead."

Freddie stops too. "New rule," he says. "I can change the rules whenever I want," he barely finishes the sentence when he's skating toward the top of the wall again.

"Hey, no fair," I hear Jake yelling.

145

"It's Sibby's turn!" yells Hannah.

I am so mad. But I need to stop thinking about what a jerk move Freddie just made. *Stay focused*, I remind myself.

Freddie is back at the top of the wall with his board over the coping. He turns his shoulders frontside. "Frontside rock n' roll," he yells.

Jackson Jo did a video on her channel about how to do this trick. It's a lot more fun than backside because you get to twist your body.

People are cheering as Freddie rides back down.

I skate up the wall. I don't let myself think about how the last time I did this trick, my back foot slipped off— just like when I try a backside bluntslide.

I think about Jackson's Jo's advice. *Keep the front foot back a little*. I turn my shoulders frontside. Rock. Kickturn really fast.

I'm on my way back down. Wind's in my face as I go.

People are cheering louder for me now than they just did for Freddie.

"SIBBY, SIBBY, SIBBY," chants fill the air.

It feels amazing.

My heart is pounding like it did the day of the competition in Charlottetown.

"My turn!" I shout at Freddie as I exit the bowl and head toward the gap.

Kickflip or 50? I can't decide. I try to remember if I saw Freddie do either when Charlie Parker Drysdale showed me the videos of him.

No, I tell myself. *Stop thinking about what Freddie can or can't do. This is about what I can do.*

I come to a full stop and stare at the wooden ledge.

"Did she quit?" I hear someone yelling.

"You done?" shouts Freddie as he catches up with me.

"*SIBBY, SIBBY, SIBBY,*" I hear from the crowd.

"What are you waiting for, Poser?" he asks.

"For you to get closer," I say.

"Huh?" he says.

"So I can tell you the next trick and you'll have lots of time to think about it," I say.

"What is it?" he asks.

"Backside bluntslide." I push as hard as I can and head toward the ledge.

"Bail before the slide and you lose!" I hear Freddie yell after me.

"If we both land it, it comes down to whoever slides the longest," I shout as I go.

Then I hear Pops. He's here. He's yelling, "*JUST SKATE!*"

I want to look up, but I don't. I need to stay focused. I'm almost at the ledge when I hear the music stop. Jake is yelling, "No, man. Come on."

I scan the crowd and see Nan, Pops, Jake, Hannah, Esther, and Charlie Parker Drysdale. Mr. MacDonald is there, too. Everyone is either frowning or yelling. I hear the sound of Freddie's skateboard getting louder and louder. I turn my head to look behind me, but just as I do, Freddie goes zipping by.

He cuts me off. He totally snaked me, and then he ollies and lands in the middle of the ledge. He's sliding.

One Mississippi. Freddie's off the ledge.

BAM. He lands.

"No. Don't do that," Jake is yelling and waving his arms at Freddie. "You're no snake."

"Why do you keep taking her side?" shouts Freddie at Jake.

"Fair is fair," yells Jake. "That wasn't cool, dude. You're better than this."

Freddie ignores Jake and stares at me. "Don't bail a third time, Poser," he says.

I must have a surprised look on my face because then he says, "What? Didn't think I'd figure out that video came from you and not Jake?"

"How'd you know?" I ask.

"There's no way he would've stopped the video before seeing if you either made the trick or bailed."

Freddie's right. And I feel even worse for messing with Jake's video. I mean, I did something I knew I shouldn't have all because I was afraid to lose. And it didn't change anything. It just made me feel like…well…not me.

"SIBBY! SIBBY!" Everyone is cheering.

That's it. I'm not letting Freddie or the things I'm afraid of get inside my head. Not anymore. I may not be chill and I may not be able to avoid trouble, but board or no board, I'm a skateboarder.

I try to block out the cheering and refocus. I don't look all the way up, but from the corner of my eye I see Esther and Hannah jumping up and down and I see a pacing yellow sweater-vest.

Freddie landed in the middle of the ledge. If I'm going to slide longer, I need to land closer to this end of it.

I skate back to where I need to go to get up enough speed. Someone turned the music back up and between that and the cheering, I can't hear much of anything.

I head toward the ledge and I pop the tail and slam it into the bluntslide position.

Back trucks are on the ledge and most of my weight is on my back foot. It doesn't slip down this time. I'm sliding.

"SIBBY, SIBBY…OH YEAH…DOPE…SICK… NO WAY…"

I feel the board underneath me, supporting me as I go.

Hold. Just go with it.

One Mississippi.

Stay balanced. Concentrate.

Hold.

Two Mississippi.

I'm off the ledge.

BAM!

I land. I'm back on the ground. My arms fly straight into the air as I skate away.

"I did it!" I yell. "I actually did it."

I look up. Jake, Hannah, Charlie Parker Drysdale, and Esther are all jumping up and down, and so are the rest of the people watching, even Mr. MacDonald. Nan, too.

She's waving at me and Pops is blowing his nose and wiping his eyes. They're wearing their matching swishy suits.

I take a deep breath and skate back up to where I was standing when I did my drop-in.

"Sibby, that was amazing," says Hannah.

"*That* was *THE BEST* thing I've *ever* seen—since my dinosaur replica anyway," says Charlie Parker Drysdale.

"Copy," says Hannah.

"Replica," says Charlie Parker Drysdale.

"*Dude*," I hear Jake's voice from behind me. "Serious respect." He lifts his fist in the air and I do the same until mine hits his.

Freddie is walking toward me.

"Fair and square," he says and passes me his board. "Take it."

"Keep it," I say. "I don't need your board any more than you need my shoes."

"Deal's a deal," says Freddie and he drops his board in front of me. He keeps his head down and runs back toward the school.

Everyone is cheering and congratulating me. Nan gives me a hug and says we're going to go back home and order pizza.

"With pepperoni," says Pops.

"But..." says Charlie Parker Drysdale.

"And we'll order a pizza Margherita too," says Nan.

He and Esther start cheering again. But, I'm watching Freddie run away and it sort of makes it feel like what just happened is the opposite of winning.

Jake says he's going to catch up with Freddie. "Maybe he'll want to hang out at my place. Later." He waves.

"Later." I wave back.

Charlie Parker Drysdale, Hannah, and Esther talk about me winning all the way to my grandparents' house. They're walking with Pops and telling him the story as if he hadn't even been there. He just keeps nodding and smiling.

Nan is telling me how proud she is.

"But I've done all of those tricks before," I say.

Nan stops walking, bends down, and looks me in the eye. "Not at that park. Not in front of that crowd and not with so many things on your mind," she says. "It takes courage to do what you did."

"I figured something out," I tell her. "And there's something I need to do before I can eat pizza."

"What?" she asks.

I whisper in Nan's ear.

She nods and says, "We won't eat until you get back."

I start to run back toward the school.

"Sibby," calls Nan.

I stop and turn.

"I am proud of my brave and smart granddaughter," she says. "But I am most proud of that mighty heart of yours."

Now I feel like I've won something.

CHAPTER 18

Making Things Right

As I get closer to the school, I try to picture the house Jake said he lived in. He said it was brown and on the other side of the empty lot.

It sure feels weird to be walking instead of skateboarding, especially since I have Freddie's skateboard in my hand. But riding it would be wrong, which is weird since I rode his other board even before he did.

When I reach the side of the school, I look past the empty lot for a brown house. All I can think about is that I need to make things right. I need to go to Jake's and find Freddie and give him back his board.

I stop walking when I see someone sitting on a skateboard in the middle of the weedy pavement. It's Freddie.

I decide I'd better not sneak up on him so I drop the board and let the sound tell him I'm behind him.

He turns and stands up. His face softens a bit when he sees me.

"Guess Jake didn't find you," I say.

"Was he looking?" asks Freddie.

"Totally," I say.

Freddie shrugs. "You come to rub it in?"

"Sorry about your grandpa," I say.

He doesn't say anything. He just looks down at his skateboard. It's the one his grandfather gave him.

"Super dope," I say and I point to the board.

He smiles. "Yep."

"You gonna ride it?" I ask.

"Guess so, since you won my other one," he says.

"Here." I push his old board toward him with my foot.

"What're you doing? You won," he says.

"Maybe you would've held the slide longer another day. Besides, if my pops died, I wouldn't have been able to skate the way I know I can skate, you know?" I say.

"Whatever," he says. "I bailed. That was the rule."

"I don't like rules," I say.

Freddie smiles a little.

"You being nice because my grandpa died?" he asks.

"Maybe. I dunno about that. I just know I want a do over," I say.

"Forget it," says Freddie and he pushes the board back in my direction. "Everyone saw me bail. Probably all think I'm a poser now."

"Posers don't skate like you just did," I say. "Seriously.

154

You're no poser. And you can always show how good you are by getting back on your board. And now you have two again 'cause I'm not keeping this one," I say, and I push the board back at him—but harder so it goes past him.

He doesn't reach for it. "It can just stay out here then, 'cause I'm not taking it either," he says.

"Suit yourself." I start to walk away.

"Hey," yells Freddie. "Did you see how all my friends were cheering for you? I mean, seriously."

"They were cheering for both of us," I say. "But the thing is…" I start. And then I realize that Vera wasn't exactly right about making friends. It's not all about being chill. "…It's about being nice. And that's hard when you're not feeling chill. I get it, but you have to keep trying."

"If I ask you something, will you promise not to tell anyone?" he says.

"Guess so," I say and start to walk back to Freddie.

"Promise," he says. "Serious. I mean I really called you out today, but I need you to promise. Skater to skater."

"Promise," I tell him. "Skater to skater."

"Does *everyone* think I turned into a mean bully?"

"Mostly." I nod.

"Do you?" he asks.

"Everyone says you changed over the summer," I say.

"I did, too. So, what I really think is that we're both scared of the same thing."

I wait for Freddie to tell me there's no way he's scared of anything, but he doesn't.

"What?" he asks.

"Changes," I say. "My changes are way different from yours, but changes are hard, especially the ones you've had. They can make you mad and sad and then mad all over again. I know. I've been mad ever since I found out we were moving and then I got really mad after I broke my board."

"Whoa," says Freddie. "You broke your board. How?"

"You won't tell?" I ask him.

"Nope," he says.

"Promise," I say. "Skater to skater."

"Promise."

"I was doing an ollie in the driveway at our old house. I cracked the deck. Lame. I mean it wasn't even when I was doing a super dope trick. I tried to patch it with glue and Popsicle sticks, but then the guy came to tell us that someone bought our house. And I just got mad and slammed my back foot down on it and it snapped. I can't believe I broke my own board. I've had it forever and *I* broke it in half. So now I don't have one, and we can't afford a new one. Serves me right."

Freddie starts laughing.

"What's so funny?" I ask. "You laugh after I tell you all that?"

"No, no," he says. "Not laughing at that exactly. I'm laughing because you snapped your foot down on your board and broke the one thing you wouldn't want to break. Doesn't make sense. It's like not riding the board my grandpa gave me. I mean I don't know why not riding this board makes me think he'll…"

Freddie drops his head. And then his head starts bobbing up and down.

I let Freddie cry.

When he stops, I help the best way I know how.

"Hey, you want come over? For pepperoni pizza?" I ask.

CHAPTER 19
It Takes More Than Once

It's been a whole week since Freddie and I played his version of S.K.A.T.E. He and Jake are staring at Jake's phone when Hannah, Charlie Parker Drysdale, Esther, and I get to the skateboard park. There is a bunch of guys standing behind him. They must be watching something amazing because none of them are skateboarding.

"Serious?" says one boy.

"Totally," says Jake. "Look."

They're all smiling, even Freddie.

And then they start high-fiving each other and all of them except Jake and Freddie disappear into the bowl.

"Hey, come look. Jackson Jo is reviewing another video Jake took of me," says Freddie.

"No way," I say. "Let's see." I walk toward him and Jake, but the others don't. "Aren't you guys coming?" I ask.

"No," says Hannah. She is standing on Esther's scooter ready to ride around the park.

158

"Maybe later," says Esther.

Charlie Parker Drysdale shakes his head.

"What's with them?" asks Freddie. "I was nice the night we had pizza."

"Takes more than once," I say.

Freddie walks closer to Hannah, Esther, and Charlie Parker Drysdale.

"Um, okay," says Freddie. "Charlie, your sweater-vest. It's dope, dude. Come see the video. And not because I'm in it. You can see Jackson Jo. She has blue hair *and* she wears glasses and gets really good grades in school."

They all look at one another.

"Come on," he says again. And then he sounds all chill and says, "Please."

They walk to Freddie and Jake, and Jake passes his phone to Esther and presses play.

"No slo-mo," he says. "Goes right into heelkick, kick-flip…and then a super dope pop shove it."

"Can you just show us Jackson Jo?" asks Esther.

"Yeah," says Hannah. "Cut to her."

"Hey, Sibby," says Freddie, as Jake starts fast-forwarding. "You wanna skate?"

"You know I don't have a board," I say.

"You can borrow mine," says Jake.

"Or," says Freddie. "Take this one. You can use it until

you get a new one." He passes me his old board and holds up the one his grandpa gave him.

"Time to take this one for a ride," he says.

"Cool," I say, and I lift my fist to bump Freddie's. I like it when skateboarders help each other out.

I put Freddie's old board down and step on.

He and I stand back to back on our boards at the top of the ramp.

"Ready?" I shout.

"Ready," he shouts back.

"One...two..."

"Hey," says Esther. "Are you guys gonna compete again? Now?"

"Yeah, are you?" asks Jake.

"Do you care?" Freddie asks.

"Nope," I say. "I just want to skate."

"Me too," he says.

And that's just what we do.

"...three," I say, and we're off.

CHAPTER 20
Go Again

Mom and Dad are sitting at the kitchen table when I get home.

"I thought you weren't coming until later," I say after I give them both a hug.

"Being away from you for a week was hard," says Mom. "We left as soon as we could because we couldn't wait to see our girl."

"Where are Nan and Pops?" I ask.

"Upstairs," says Dad. "Your mom and I need to talk to you."

"Oh, no. Are we moving again?" I ask.

"No, Sibby. We're staying here for a while," says Dad.

"Honey," Mom starts, "Nan and Pops say you broke your skateboard."

"Why didn't you tell us?" Dad asks.

"It's not like we can afford a new one," I answer.

"That's not the point," says Mom. "We always want to know what's going on with you. You know that."

Dad reaches under the table and pulls out a skateboard that looks a lot like my old one.

"*What*…?" I reach for the board. "Wait! I broke it. How…?"

"Turns out Vera got a new one, so we bought her old one," says Dad.

"We thought it might remind you of skateboarding with her," says Mom.

"I won't break this one," I say. "No way."

"Well, if you do," says Dad. "You need to tell us."

"Sibby, we want you to keep skateboarding. You're so good. We'll do whatever we can to help make that happen," says Mom.

"But we had to sell all our stuff, even the house."

"You let us worry about money," Mom says.

"You can't stop doing what you love," says Dad.

"Then why did you?" I ask him. "I mean you loved building houses. But then you quit."

"It was time for a change," he says.

"Dad," I say. "Come on."

"Jason," says Mom. "I think she's on to you."

Dad looks at me, "So okay, busted. We moved because—"

"Because you quit when you lost your confidence all because of a bully," I blurt out.

"What?" asks Dad.

"Who told you that?" Mom wants to know.

"I heard you talking," I say. "And then we started selling everything."

"Sib," says Dad. "It's good to stand up to a bully, but you also need to know when it's time to put your energy somewhere else, somewhere more important. I left my job because your mom and I decided it was one of those times. And I have an opportunity for a job somewhere else."

"Where?" I ask.

"Out West," he says. "I'll be gone for a few weeks but then home for a few weeks. Your mom and I wanted you both to be closer to Nan and Pops until we know for sure whether or not this even works. Nothing is for sure."

"You're going to live there?" I ask. "For weeks?"

"It's temporary," he says.

"And I have a job interview at an office downtown next week," says Mom. "Honey, changes are part of life. It's all about how you look at them. Let's look at this as an opportunity. Not many kids get to live with grandparents who love them so much."

"I know," I say. "And I have my skateboard back."

"Enjoy it because tomorrow starts a week of no skate-boarding," says Mom.

"*What?*" I say.

"No helmet?" she says. "Really?"

"CHARLIE PARKER DRYSDALE!" I shout.

"Hey," says Dad. "He was right to say something. Sibby, you can't go fooling with your safety. And you can't go breaking promises to your mom and me because you're mad. Got it?"

"Yeah," I mutter. "I do."

"Hey down there. Can we have dinner soon?" yells Pops from upstairs.

"Come on down, Dad," Mom says and walks out of the kitchen.

Dad starts to follow her.

"Hey, Dad, wait," I say.

He stops. "What is it?"

"I'm sorry I was so mad at you before. I mean, I didn't know why I was mad at first, but I do now."

"Well, that's great," he says. "Tell me. What'd I do?"

"It's not what you did. It's what happened. Changes are scary."

"I'm sorry, Sibby," he says. He stops looking me in the eye and looks down at the floor. "I never want you to be unhappy. And not the kind of unhappy you feel when

164

I ask you to put your bike in the garage. I mean really unhappy."

"But I'm not," I tell him. "Living here is different, but it's good."

"Sibby, you have no idea how glad I am to hear that." He looks me in the eye again.

"One more thing," I say. "Doubting can make you lose confidence, no matter how straight you stand up."

Dad smiles. "It sure can."

"Pops says the secret is up here." I point to my forehead. "He says, when you start doubting, you start losing. You're good at building houses. Keep thinking about that. It'll be okay."

"You're super dope smart, you know that?" he says, and we high five.

I put my helmet and pads on and take my skateboard outside and ride it up and down the sidewalk in front of Nan and Pop's house. As I'm riding, pictures pop into my head, but not the same ones as before. I don't see Vera's sad face saying good-bye, Dad's sad face selling our tent, or my broken skateboard.

I see all the changes and how they turned out okay. I see Nan and Pop's kitchen table, me eating pepperoni pizza with Freddie while Charlie Parker Drysdale, Hannah, and Esther eat pizza Margherita, me laughing with my friends, bumping fists with Jake, skateboarding at the new skatepark, Pops passing me my lunch in the nice new bag he bought that's an actual lunch bag, Nan's hugs.

I ride along the sidewalk and see a weed.

I decide to ollie over it, but change my mind at the last minute and do a kickflip.

I trip on the landing, bail, and land on Charlie Parker Drysdale's front lawn right on my backside.

"Hey, was that a slam?" I hear him call from the front window of his house.

"No," I say. "Not even close. It didn't hurt. How long have you been watching?" I ask.

"Just saw the part where you fell," he says. "I'm coming out."

I watch Charlie Parker Drysdale close the window and disappear inside his house before coming out his front door. I roll over on my side and look back at that weed.

"Get back up and go again," I hear a voice say.

But it's not Vera's voice, or Freddie's, or Nan's, or Pop's, or Charlie Parker Drysdale's, or anyone else's.

It's mine.

"You got this," it tells me. And I know I do.

So I get back up.

And I go again.

Acknowledgments

A heartfelt thanks to the team at Second Story Press. Your knowledge and expertise have shone through in each and every interaction, as have your professionalism, kindness, and enthusiasm. Thank you for making this experience everything I had hoped working with a publishing team would be. And a special thank you for creating a cover that makes my heart do an ollie!

For Sophia and Maya Ashley-Martin, two of the coolest kids I know. I asked for your expert opinion on my manuscript, which you gave without hesitation. And look what happened. That manuscript became a book. Thank you! Thanks also to Sophia and Maya's mom, Jillian. I am so grateful for our friendship, for our chats, and for your willingness to read and comment on *Sibby* in all her versions.

Thank you to my friends Janet Barlow, Heather Breeze, Christine Chantegreil, and Nadia Stuewer for your help and encouragement. And a thank you to donalee Moulton for your ear, edits, and enthusiasm. Thanks also to the Canadian Society of Authors, Illustrators, and Performers (CANSCAIP); the Society of Canadian Book Writers and Illustrators (SCBWI); and the Writers' Federation of Nova Scotia (WFNS). The conferences I've attended and the workshops I've taken have been tremendously helpful and have provided important networking opportunities. A special note of thanks to Alma Fullerton and the team at SCBWI Canada East. It was at a conference you hosted that I first introduced *Sibby* and where I met Lynn Leitch. Lynn, you are a trusted friend and a wonderful writer. I've learned so much from you. I also want to thank Heather Alexander for reminding me what stories like Sibby's need to be and do. I loved working with you.

And now for the people who fill my world with love: my family. A big thanks to Mike for your ongoing encouragement, for all the writing magazines and books you've given me over the years, and for always being there. To my sister and cheerleader, Colleen. Thank you for all those reminders that "rejection is part of the path." I've always appreciated your wisdom and your desire to deliver a confidence boost. Thanks to John and Jean for being so thoughtful and for your willingness to help in whatever way possible. Special thanks go to my parents, Don and Mary O'Connor. You are the inspiration for Sibby's loving and humorous grandparents—and their matching tracksuits! Thank you for encouraging me to read, to write, to dream, and to skateboard. And finally, my complete, knows-no-end gratitude to Meredith. You are the hardest one to thank because "thank you" hardly seems enough. You and Olivia are my inspiration and a dream come true.

About the Author

CLARE O'CONNOR is a communications professional and writer. She fell in love with skateboarding at the age of seven and practiced tricks on the dead-end street where she grew up. She now lives in Halifax, Nova Scotia with her family and still owns a skateboard. *Skateboard Sibby* is her first novel.